Acclaim for *The Lord's Motel*

"This is what, beneath its hilarious surface, *The Lord's Motel* is about: Is it possible to find goodness and happiness in the world we inhabit today? *The Lord's Motel* answers in the affirmative.... It brings back our own younger, crazy days and leaves us laughing, holding hope in our hands. It is a treasure."
—Susan Fromberg Schaeffer, *Chicago Sun-Times*

"Wonderful descriptions of Houston, its funky sections and its people...a savvy portrait of single men and women and the nightmare that is dating in the 1990s."
—Judyth Rigler, *San Antonio Express-News*

"Gail Donohue Storey mourns 'absent lovers, absent fathers, absent gods' with equal passion, and in her search she turns up a wonderful cast of fellow-sufferers.... I kept wishing Colleen were real—witty, honest, and open, she'd make a terrific friend. Or maybe (as Holden Caulfield suggested) after a really bad day you could call up Storey herself and let her put her own special twist on your predicament simply by retelling it in her own dazzled, vulnerable, and knowing voice."
—Rosellen Brown

"An entertaining read and a winning debut for Gail Donohue Storey."
—McCoy C. Campbell, *Chattanooga Times*

"Blisteringly funny and impossibly wise. Set in cranky, surprising Houston, [*The Lord's Motel*] is local all right, yet resounds out to touch at the nervous uncertainty a lot of Americans, particularly American women, are feeling right now."
—Beverly Lowry

"Gail Donohue Storey...keeps *The Lord's Motel* moving quickly with her funny insights and quirky sense of humor.... A sharp eye for social detail also informs it."
—Holly Hildebr

"A hilarious and poignant first novel about love, the singles scene, and the absurdities of modern life.... A lively and eccentric cast of characters, an off-beat plot, and a spunky heroine make for light and enjoyable reading."
—*Library Journal*

"Wonderful people and a tart, upbeat story set against a Houston backdrop that captures the heat and heart of the city.... a first-rate first novel."
—*Amarillo News-Globe*

"Echoes of *Looking for Mr. Goodbar*.... Colleen is a sympathetic and ironic character."
—Michael Bauman, *Milwaukee Journal*

"Storey pokes light-hearted fun at the foibles of urban Texas.... though her prose seems light as meringue, Storey has deeper aims. The antics of her characters raise some important issues."
—John Herndon, *Austin American-Statesman*

"Storey's novel is written with an eye for precise detail.... Colleen is such an engaging narrator."
—David Theis, *Houston Press*

"I like *The Lord's Motel* quite a lot.... There's something right about the book's effort to find a way for a woman not to hyperbolize about women and men in modern times, but to talk straight, to go from the shoulder, to see us all as people rather than position papers. Embarked on this wise and admirable, and humane, agenda, *The Lord's Motel* never forgets its roots, its heart, or its wicked tongue."
—Frederick Barthelme

THE
LORD'S MOTEL

Gail Donohue Storey

PERSEA BOOKS   NEW YORK

ACKNOWLEDGMENTS

I wish to thank James Stafford, Deborah Keyser, Lieutenant David Burke, Sergeant Allen Rogers, and Barbara Belbot for their help with research for this novel, as well as Eugene Boisaubin, M.D., and Diane Wasden, M.D. For their encouragement and support I thank Porter Storey, M.D., Warren J. Gustus, Jan Short, Tracy Daugherty, Karen Braziller, Yaddo, and the Virginia Center for the Creative Arts.

For information, write to the publisher:
Persea Books, Inc.
60 Madison Avenue
New York, New York 10010

Library of Congress Cataloging-in-Publication Data

Storey, Gail Donohue.
    The Lord's motel / Gail Donohue Storey.
        p.   cm.
    ISBN 0-89255-194-1
    I. Title.
    PS3569.T6487L67   1992
    813'.54—dc20   92-10532

Designed by Semadar Megged
Typeset in Sabon by Keystrokes, Lenox, Massachusetts
Printed and bound by Haddon Craftsmen, Scranton, Pennsylvania
First paperback printing

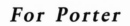

For Porter

CONTENTS

THE LORD'S MOTEL

1

Service-to-the-Unserved

Is it better to have fun with a kinky man or to be gloomy with a good one? Should I try to find someone to love who's no more fun than I am, or should I stick with Web Desiderio since there's no one out there anyway? Web's the social director on a cruise ship. He dances his way through the Panama Canal, swims up to the swim-up bar on the Upper Nile, plays "Kiss the Pirate" in the waters of Aruba, Bora-Bora, Pulau Pangkor. I don't see him often but he keeps alive in me the illusion that I'm in a relationship while he doesn't have to relate to me that much.

I'm sitting at my desk in the administrative offices of the public library worrying about my love for Web when Lucille, the secretary, buzzes me.

"You have a call on line one, Colleen," she says. I can see her smirk over the phone.

"I read in the newspaper that your jail prohibits lingerie," Web says when I pick up the receiver. He sounds far away but there's no point in asking where. He'd tell me he's on a ship in the Caribbean when he's on a pay phone around the corner. Our love life is just like that.

"It's not my jail, I just deliver library books to it," I say.

"The federal lawsuit says jail officials won't let male prisoners wear interesting underwear," he goes on, "and females have to surrender the underwires in their bras."

"I don't deliver underwear," I say.

"I just thought you'd want to know," he says. "Are you wearing lingerie right now?"

"Of course," I say.

He whispers incorrigible nothings in my ear. The kinkier he talks the fainter he sounds. Anyway, I hang up on him because I'm trying to transform myself from a tart on a heroic quest into a handmaiden of higher consciousness.

Actually, I'm desperate. Jobs, not men, come looking for me. I got every job I ever applied for, even ones I never applied for, because prospective employers sense immediately that the place I hold in my family-of-origin is The Rescuer. "You've got to start earning a living," my mother told me when I was ten. I've been working ever since.

Joanne, the library director, is an Idea Woman. She spotted me immediately as someone who could implement her ideas because I'm so organized and eager to please. The Service-to-the-Unserved project was my idea but she's still perfectly happy to let me implement it as long as it makes her look good. Joanne is big and brassy with platinum flyaway hair, in her early fifties, of unpredictable temper. She has the hostility of the fat for the thin, so basically I try not to remind her of my existence except by monthly reports in her in-box. She likes to know what's going on—not the problems, but how I solved them. She's not that great an administrator but she is a great bully.

Today I'm on Joanne's good side because she's showing off Service-to-the-Unserved to the Board of Trustees. I'm giving my slide presentation with running commentary of hard facts, cold figures, and warm, human feeling for the needs of the community. I'm in the Board Room, arranging my slides in the carousel, when the Trustees start arriving.

"Hah, how're yew?" one of them says to another, sticking out his hand. It's code for How High Are You—on what executive level and on how much booze. They can't talk and they can't write; women with Ph.D.s in English are back in their offices writing their letters and speeches for them. The women read the newspapers and press releases and figure out how to respond, to save the respective executive faces. Later this afternoon the women will sit on the sofas in the executive offices, putting words in the men's mouths so they'll get the gist of how they're supposed to think.

The Trustees like Joanne because she's a fundraising type. "Leave out the slides of the jail," she whispers hoarsely to me as she barrels by.

Prisoners are not politically popular, never mind library service for them. The jail officials are afraid the inmates will use paperbacks to stop up the toilets and cause a riot. But everyone has cultural guilt about older adults, so I put in more of my nursing home slides, followed by homebound people reading in their beds and kids who said yes to drugs watching library films at the psychiatric hospital.

The Trustees are in their seats with their coffee and pow-dered-sugar doughnuts.

"Is library service for *everyone?*" I say, and begin my presentation with a slide of Mrs. Fritz, my first homebound patron, frail with illness but overjoyed at her stack of mysteries. There's something very festive about it after all, *Moby-Dick* and *The Great Gatsby* in Large Print editions for the visually-impaired, Hemingway for a businessman at home after a stroke, thrillers for the nursing homes, rap discs for the hospitalized adolescents. In the slides, the people look startled but happy to be getting such personal attention from the library. I end the show with a slide of me jauntily driving the bright blue Service-to-the-Unserved van west into the sunset.

When the lights come back on, I refer the Trustees to the information packet I've put at each of their places—budget, circulation statistics, homebound population estimates, plans for future programming, publicity clippings, the service brochure.

"But is it cost-effective?" one of them asks.

"Not only is it cost-effective," I say, "it's attracting tax dollars to the library through publicity, good will, and increased library use."

There wasn't a dry eye in the audience during my slide show, I think, calculating how I'm going to expand the prisoners' library service.

Joanne looks pleased. "Colleen, there wasn't a dry eye in the audience during your slide show," she says when they've all left.

It's lunchtime, and I dash off to the health club for my aerobic dance class. This is our real rush hour—the club is full of us, flashing our plastic membership cards as we whip through the turnstile, dash through the downstairs locker room. I race upstairs to the gleaming gym in my hot-pink leotard with high-cut hips, shiny black tights, my waist cinched with a black and silver sash. The women in the class dress for success, as do the gay men in their red, black, silver briefs and leg-warmers. Only the straight men and older women wear the white T-shirts and boxer shorts provided by the club.

We each take our favorite spot on the floor, do stretches, while Suzi, our teacher, plugs in her microphone and slips the disco music into the system, turns on the strobe lights. She hops around in her designer leotard; today it's a glittery turquoise. What's it like to have your work clothes be leotards and tights with coordinated headbands, legwarmers, shoelaces? "I spent six thousand dollars on leotards last year," she confided to me once after class. Of course, they're write-offs.

I bend over and touch my toes, look between my knees at the others. I look at the world upside down at least once a day. The aerobic angels are running in place and walking on the ceiling, weightless, floating. They're continuous with one another. We're all going to move, we're all going to move at the same time, to the same place.

Suzi's job is to channel all our frenetic efficiency into bouncy, happy, aerobic dancing. "Are you *Ready?*" she whoops. "For some *Fun?!*" And we're off, one hundred of us high-kicking, jumping-jacking, doing triple turns and crossovers like desperate cheerleaders. She turns up the music and the women's makeup runs with sweat, the men's jockstraps show through their damp shorts. She gets us going, flirts with the lawyers and accountants dancing without imagination. She runs and leaps, we follow, while she chants breathy instructions into her microphone. Our thighs glow pink. Worrying about my life and achievements, I remind myself I've made it to a Level Three aerobic dance class.

After high- and low-impact we do arm work with our hand weights—yuppie toys. Then we do floor work—inner or outer thighs or quads or abs. The women always want to do hamstrings for our cellulite, but the men pout and leave halfway thought the set.

"You'll be lopsided," Suzi yells after them.

I like the cool-down stretches because Suzi turns down the lights and it's the closest thing to a low stimulation environment any of us is likely to get in this life or the next.

"Please, please, *please* tell all the songwriters you know no more ten-sixes," Suzi says through her mike while we put away our mats.

"What's she talking about?" I ask the woman next to me.

"Beats," she says. "Haven't you noticed we're okay as long as the music has four-eight counts?"

"No," I say. "I'm verbal, not quantitative."

After class everyone disperses immediately to shower and get back to his desk. Some people don't even stay for the cool-down. It's not good form to ask anyone's name. The men are afraid they'd be accused of rape for even talking to us. No one knows where anyone works.

The club provides everything—shampoo and rinse, towels, disposable paper shoes for the shower. I look longingly toward the sauna and whirlpool and the tiny ultraviolet tanning room, but I have too much guilt not to tear back to the office. I have it down to a science of small motions—my locker's combination, toweling myself dry down one side and up the other, putting on my hosiery with one hand and my makeup with the other. I save twenty seconds by just leaving on my earrings.

Sometimes, standing alone in the row where my locker is, I start to cry for no reason. Standing dressed in front of my open locker with my high heels in my hand, I can't remember whether I'm on my way to class or ready to leave because it's over.

This afternoon I'm meeting for the third time with Lieutenant Sprunt, overseer of the jail, to try to persuade him that his prisoners need library service. I drive there in the blue Service-to-the-Unserved van. Smaller than a bookmobile but bigger than my VW bug, the van gives me the bravado I need to get on Houston's autobahn. My terror accelerates on the entrance ramp. I crane my neck every which way around the blind spots, trying not to crash into someone in front because that would automatically make it my fault. Then I have to undo my terror getting off the exit ramp, merging with a string of frantic cars getting on.

Lieutenant Sprunt is not overly fond of me. Library service is just another headache to him. He's a classic obstructionist, with the smashed-in face of a Fu dog. I'll just keep coming back until I become more of a headache than library service would be.

"The security problems are insurmountable," he says.

"Surely not for you," I say.

"These guys are animals," he says. "They'll destroy library property in unmentionable ways, even use the books as weapons."

"Books are weapons against ignorance, prisoners have the Right to Read," I say, leaning so far to the left I nearly fall off my chair.

"Most of 'em can't read," he says.

"The library has magazines, books of photographs, travel books with pictures," I say. "Why don't we try limited service to a selected group of inmates with good behavior records?"

"Tell you what," he sighs. "We'll try it, but only on the ladies. Who knows, it might be an incentive to the trouble-makers to clean up their acts. Send Dolores up here," he growls into the intercom on his desk.

"Delighted to meet you," I say, extending my hand when a woman in a tan jail-issue jumpsuit walks into Lieutenant Sprunt's office. She's accompanied by a female corrections officer in blue who stands at the door and folds her arms across her chest.

Dolores is one of those women whose lives are so harsh they look older than they are, but are too young to have the grown children they invariably have. I, on the other hand, look younger than thirty-one because I haven't yet performed certain life tasks. Dolores wears glasses with cheap frames, one bow Scotch-taped to the eyepiece. Her squat body is out of shape, her skin the pasty color of non-dairy creamer. I get better at makeup as I look older and more awful. To stay a perfect henna, I'm putting my hairdresser's kids through college. Dolores's wild brown hair has a hint of red in it, like dry underbrush about to burst into flames.

Lieutenant Sprunt doesn't invite her to sit down. She looks frightened. Lieutenant Sprunt hems and haws as if he doesn't know how to broach the subject. "Dolores," he says finally, "can you read?"

"Yes, sir," she says almost inaudibly, breathing a sigh of relief.

"This little lady," Lieutenant Sprunt goes on, cocking his head toward me, "wants to bring books from the public library every month."

Dolores steals a look at me. I smile encouragingly but she quickly looks back down at the floor.

"You'll see that the books get passed out to the inmates, then returned," Lieutenant Sprunt says. "Can you do that, Dolores?"

"No complicated record-keeping is necessary," I say, seeing the terror in Dolores's eyes. "The service will be informal and if the materials don't come back we'll assume they're being used."

"See that they're returned, Dolores," Lieutenant Sprunt says.

"Yes, sir," Dolores says.

The corrections officer at the door snorts. I take out my outline of the collection and start checking it off like a take-out menu.

"A basic collection for our initial visit," I go on, "might include a broad selection of current magazines, contemporary fiction, some how-to and self-help books, vocational manuals, mystery and romance paperbacks, a few law reference books, some biographies, that sort of thing. Do you have additional suggestions, Dolores?"

"No, ma'am," she says.

I don't believe her. She looks hungry. She looks as if her

entire life is a meditation on self-containment.

"Anything at all?" I say.

"Do they have any books on how to draw?" she says finally, with a flat-footed Southern accent. Her voice is hoarse with despair.

"What an excellent suggestion," I say, making a note.

"Don't get the wrong idea," Lieutenant Sprunt says to me. "We don't give them any paper or pencils or anything."

"Oh," I say. "Nevertheless..."

I sense that in Lieutenant Sprunt's view Dolores has already exceeded allowable enthusiasm. The corrections officer ambles over to escort her away.

"Thank the lady, Dolores," Sprunt says, as if he'd better order it before it happens without his permission.

"Thank you, ma'am," Dolores says, holding my eye for a moment.

The longing in her eye terrifies me. She's not only lonely but guilty, defiant, frightened, submissive, enraged.

Service-to-the-Unserved, Love to the Unloved. What could I be if not my longing? I've misspent my life up to now—up to and including longing for Web who lives on cruise ships while I live in Texas, my longing-distance lover.

"You're more than welcome, Dolores," I say. "I look forward to working with you."

2

The Lord's Motel

I drive home from the library, past the shotgun houses and soul food shacks of the Fourth Ward, into Montrose and its no-zoning hodgepodge of museums, massage parlors, gay bars, glitzy restaurants, down the shady streets of my neighborhood. When I moved here from Boston during the great Yankee yuppie migration, I expected Houston to look like the dusty towns on TV cowboy shows. It turns out that most of those were filmed in Arizona, and Houston looks more like Miami was supposed to, tropical and lush with green palmetto trees and pink crepe myrtles.

Two bushy palms shade the front of my apartment building, the Lord's Motel. St. Francis, our building manager, named it that because he says we're always driving in and out of the mind of God. I drive behind the building into the parking lot. St. Francis waves from the kitchen window of his rear apartment. He's standing at his kitchen sink, washing carrots, working his juicer. He always watches for us, coming home from our jobs to the Lord's Motel—me, Gigi, then Barbara. As our building manager, he keeps in balance this particular part of the mind of God. He listens for the workings of that mind—the snap of a branch as a squirrel lands on it, our car tires on the pavement, a man hammering on a piece of wood in a neighboring yard.

St. Francis pours carrot juice into a jelly jar for me, in case I was thinking of a Bloody Mary. I stand in his kitchen and sip at it. Together we watch Gigi drive into her parking space in her little silver BMW. She waves at us and starts talking before she's out of the car. She must be talking to us because there's no one else in the parking lot but the cats and a few scraggly birds. Gigi and I were best friends at a girls' high school in Boston—Our Lady of Perpetual Sorrows. We went our separate ways to college and graduate school, then found each other again at our tenth high school reunion. In the meantime, she'd married and divorced a CPA named Henry. She followed me to Houston and the Lord's Motel to get as far away from Henry as possible. I've never met him, but I feel I know him intimately as the quintessential stuffed shirt. Gigi's making a new life for herself selling computer software and dating another software salesman named Jack.

Gigi balances an open can of Coke on the car roof and yanks her purse and shopping bags out of the front seat. Tiny, with chic black hair, she comes in and hugs St. Francis, who hugs her back with humility. He looks puzzled to get a hug from each of us every evening, but Gigi started it and now we all do it.

"What a day," Gigi says. "I was speeding on the transitway to meet a client, and I ran into a construction ditch. The policeman would have given me a ticket except I told him I was on my way to church."

"The transitway is just for double occupancy vehicles," St. Francis says.

"St. Francis, it's not like I committed a *sin*," Gigi says.

Gigi's recovery from the concept of sin began sooner than

mine—with high school dating, I think. I dated a little too, if you can call it that; I took the boy next door to my high school dances until he went into the seminary. I took a boy named Stephen after that, until he also went into the seminary. Each believed I was an "occasion of sin," trying to tempt him to kiss or hold hands. I heard they each left the priesthood eventually, but by then I was already far down the road to ruin. Gigi doesn't worry anymore about the flesh vs. spirit conflict, while I'm still floundering in the wreckage of mine.

"Did you get hurt?" I ask Gigi.

"I could have been crackerjack city," she says, "but my biggest concern is I trashed my Ferragamos."

"Care for a little carrot juice?" St. Francis asks her.

"God, no," Gigi says, swigging at her Coke.

"Sugar makes you crazy," St. Francis says.

Gigi laughs and trips up the stairs. She's in No. 5, as in Chanel, right above St. Francis and across the hall from me.

"What do you hear about our eyebrow mousse?" she calls back down the stairs.

"Our refills haven't come in yet," I say.

Gigi isn't that much more materialistic than I am; she just likes to make a big thing of it in front of St. Francis. She thinks it's unhealthy to live in such a New Age atmosphere so she tries to overcompensate. She's a borderline vegetarian, but she smokes.

St. Francis goes back to his carrots. Out in the parking lot, the cats stalk a pigeon; it escapes in a flurry of feathers to the roof of the carport. The cats are hanging around the back step, acting as if it's suppertime. St. Francis has been feeding them just in the mornings for a year now and they still expect to eat again at supper.

"Morning, feed the cats, evening, hug you girls," St. Francis says to me.

Names don't take to the cats. The property owners, a Group, don't allow pets, but the cats don't want to live in the building. Sometimes the cats are like quiet people, careful not to bump into each other in the soft dusk. St. Francis thinks we tenants come and go more gently then, bright forms softly aware of each other. He tries to explain it to me now, over our New Age Happy Hour.

"Are you talking about individuated consciousnesses?" I say.

He looks down and goes back to sawing carrots. I gaze around his spotless apartment. All he has in his living room is his futon; his meditation cushion sits in the middle of his bedroom. St. Francis won't tell us how old he is because he says he has eternal life. I'd put him at fifty-something, a sixties kid to whom the sixties go on happening.

Barbara roars into the parking lot, her white Buick LeSabre digging tracks into the grass on both sides of the narrow driveway. The cats scatter. She climbs out with her briefcase. She's one of those blond, big-boned Texas gals who grew up on a ranch to become an international loan officer.

"A little carrot juice?" St. Francis asks Barbara.

"With a twist, please," Barbara says.

St. Francis hugs her anyway. She marches to her mailbox and comes back to sit down at St. Francis's table. She tears open her Merrill Lynch statements as if they're love letters.

"The market is going just absolutely crazy," she tells us, her nostrils flaring. "It's giving me endometriosis."

"What's endometriosis?" he asks. "Maybe I have an herb that might be good for it."

"It's being embattled by hormones without having a man to make it all worthwhile, is what it is," she says.

"Praise God," St. Francis says in wonderment.

"It's like I'm a big cow waiting for a bull to come along

and impregnate me," Barbara goes on, "but all the bulls can think about is making money, so instead my entire reproductive system is reproducing God knows what from one end of itself to the other."

"You're not a cow," St. Francis says to her. "You're a little stocky, but you're not a cow."

When Texas banks were failing and loan officers were being fired right and left, Barbara got promoted. Gigi and I concluded she's very smart. She works even harder than we do—hers is the first car out of the parking lot every morning.

"It's a jungle out there, St. Francis," she says. "You're smart to stay home and not work."

"I work," St. Francis says, a little wounded. "I paint the apartments, fix the leaky faucets, mow the grass. There's the garbage on Tuesdays and Fridays, recycling on Wednesdays. I feed the cats. I hug you girls. Praise God."

"That's about all the nurturing we're likely to get," Barbara says, and tramps down the hall. She lives in the front apartment, across the hall from Mrs. Fritz. She has furnished her apartment in country antiques—maple cupboards, quilts, baskets—so she can walk out of the banking world into the comfort of a farmhouse kitchen. We listen to Barbara's footsteps until they subside beneath the sea-volume of traffic from the Southwest Freeway. Barbara slams her door; I have a vision of hot dust rising from her old sofa.

St. Francis shakes his head. In his long gray hair and beard, he looks more like a wizard than an ascetic, just as he did when I first met him. It was August, Houston's hottest month. I'd left my job as an ordinary librarian in Boston to start Service-to-the-Unserved in Houston. I drove around looking for an apartment in the searing heat. My VW bug wasn't air-conditioned; it was like driving around in Hell. The apartments I looked at were seedy, dank with mildewed shag carpets, on arid lots. The humidity hung over everything with a deathly silence. It seemed that all the world napped in air-conditioned comfort while I wandered desolate in the emptiness of the afternoon. Sweaty and discouraged, I stopped in front of the Lord's Motel to get my bearings. St. Francis came out to see what was the matter. I told him I was apartment-hunting. "I have a vacant apartment here in the Lord's Motel," he said kindly. "The Lord told me he'd send someone today."

This alarmed me, but I couldn't resist the apartment. It's clean and airy, with smooth white walls, oak floors. Built in the fifties, it has mint-green tile in the kitchen and a Formica counter shaped like a boomerang, casement windows that open into the trees. It made me feel I could start my life over again at an earlier point in time.

Mrs. Fritz came to the Lord's Motel with the same relief I did. She comes out of her apartment now and walks down the hallway to St. Francis and me. She holds onto the wall because she's ninety-five and her balance is rocky. Her white hair makes her look like a slowly advancing cloud. She was my first Service-to-the-Unserved homebound person, living alone in an old house on lower Westheimer. It was a dangerous neighborhood of addicts and runaways. Too deaf to hear anyone knock, she kept her door open so people could just walk in—the postman, and Meals on Wheels until she decided their food was too bland. I grew fond of her, perhaps because she's how I see myself at ninety-five—alone, childless, but still feisty. All four of us helped her move into the Lord's Motel so we could keep an eye on her. Gigi and St. Francis packed things, Barbara and I did the heavy lifting, and Mrs. Fritz supervised, rocking and reeling among us.

"Cat food is on sale," she says, handing St. Francis a grocery bag. "I had it delivered." She accepts a green plastic glass of carrot juice and tells us about a dream she and Barbara both had a couple of nights ago. "It was so *vivid*," she says. "I woke up because I could feel this cat walking up my blanket toward my face? Barbara said the cat in her dream walked up *her* blanket, then jumped over her face and flew out the window."

St. Francis shifts in his chair. "Anything can happen when you're on the astral plane like that," he says.

"But how could it happen to both Barbara and me on the same night?" she says.

"Miracles begin to happen when you grow closer to God," he says.

Mrs. Fritz asks him to check a gas leak in her apartment. She always thinks she smells gas, but St. Francis never finds a leak. Mrs. Fritz may have a superior sense of smell that compensates for her hearing loss. Someday the building will blow up and it will turn out there was a gas leak after all.

I go upstairs to my own apartment.

Gigi opens her door to gossip with me across the hall, like we always do. She talks to me about Jack, the man she's seeing; I talk to her about Web, and together we rehash and interpret everything. We worry about each other. We give each other pep talks.

"Web called me today," I say. "To talk about the prisoners' underwear."

We met Web when he was being auctioned off as Most Eligible Bachelor at a Friends of the Library benefit, three years ago. He came with two tickets for a cruise to Paradise Island. We pooled our money and got him. Web was the social director on the cruise ship. He was charming to both of us, but he made me feel he'd been waiting for me on that cruise ship all his life. He treated me to champagne at the swim-up bar. He taught me to swing on the golf simulator. He was the Pirate the night I won "Kiss the Pirate."

"Prisoners' underwear!" Gigi says. "He's probably prepping you for some new fantasy."

"Why did Web choose *me* and not you to act out his fantasies?" I ask Gigi.

"Same reason the library picked you to run Service-to-the-Unserved," she says. "You have masochist written all over you."

"I have rescuer written all over me," I say.

"Same thing," she says, but I fail to see the parallel.

"If Web needs me so much, why does he flirt with other women right in front of me?" I say.

"He's testing you," she says.

"Does Jack flirt with other women in front of *you*?" I say.

Gigi laughs at the very thought. "He knows it wouldn't work on me," she says.

"Well, shit," I say.

"Goodnight, sweetie," she sighs.

I open the door to my own apartment. I hover on the threshold. The bamboo chairs are upholstered with white cabbage roses and green leaves, the tables are covered with seashells, the bookshelves crammed with green, pink, yellow spines. Mirrors, windows, leafy plants, Japanese rice paper shades. The room is on the verge of something; it wants to open up and let me through.

I stir-fry some vegetables for my supper, pour a glass of wine, and read while I eat. I live close to the sound of the fork on my plate. When I wash the dishes, they thicken in my hand. I do some ironing, try to pay close attention to the soothing intimacy of the warm iron on the soft cloth.

I hear Jack arrive at Gigi's across the hall. "It's me," he booms through her door. I hear Gigi's giggle as she lets him in.

It gets dark. I hope it won't be a bad night for the pay phone. The building owners let Southwestern Bell put a pay phone in the front yard, right outside Barbara's window. Some nights there's a steady stream of junkies, drunks, anybody who has been locked out, thrown out, or is just up to something. On those nights, Barbara comes down and bangs on St. Francis's door. "I want that phone out of there!" she cries. St. Francis always calls the Group the next morning, but he can't bring himself to talk to their answering machine. "Like praying to a graven image," he says. Once in a while he gets through to a secretary. "Everyone is out of the office," the secretary says. "I'd take a message but this isn't my desk." "Praise God," St. Francis says. He tells us that it's not what happens to us that's important, it's how we act when it's happening.

I hear Barbara banging on St. Francis's door now, but it seems too early for the trouble with the pay phone. I lean over the banister and St. Francis motions to me to come down.

Right away I can see this is a thousand-hankie cry. Barbara is awash in a sea of Kleenex. Her blue eyes are rimmed with pink, her thick blond hair in disarray.

"I'm pregnant!" she cries. "I gave myself one of those pregnancy tests."

"Who's the baby's father?" I say.

"He's a welder," Barbara cries.

"A welder!" I say. "How did you ever get to know a welder?"

"He came to use the phone," she says.

"What phone? Your phone?"

"No, the pay phone in the front yard."

"Barbara!"

"I'm sick of proximity without intimacy," she says. "I called him up out there from my phone. One thing just led to another."

"Just like with meat," St. Francis says. He thinks meat is the root of all evil.

Barbara and I stare at him.

"Being pregnant might cure your endometriosis," I say to Barbara. "Have you told the welder?"

"I'll never even see him again unless he comes back to use the phone."

"Aren't those do-it-yourself pregnancy tests for early morning?" I say.

"Oh, great," she says. "If I'm pregnant tonight, I'll be even more pregnant by tomorrow morning!"

"Don't try to decide anything tonight," I say.

Over our heads we hear Gigi moaning and calling out Jack's name.

St. Francis is karma-specific. "This wouldn't be happening," he says, "if in a past life I hadn't tormented my building manager with my noises of carnal desire."

Barbara gives a little laugh, as if St. Francis has said this to cheer her up. She pulls herself together with the composure that must have got her through the Texas banking crisis. Although her face is puffy from crying, she looks vaguely triumphant. She looks down at her abdomen, rearranges herself more comfortably, as if she can feel the baby taking hold inside of her. She dumps her Kleenex into St. Francis's wastebasket and heads back to her apartment.

I go upstairs and lie in bed to the sounds of crickets and frogs. The night grows quiet, but I can't sleep because of the buzz of a helicopter flying low over the backyards. I go downstairs in my bathrobe and peer out the front door at the pay phone, look up and down the street.

Half a block away, on the steamy sidewalk in front of a bar, six shapes are gathered around a dog. The men are laughing and making gross noises. The dog is tied up. They're doing something obscene to the dog. Hard rock blares out with the bar light. The dog barks so continuously it seems to be keeping time with the music. The lead singer has one of those yelling male voices, and the musicians are all drunk. The police arrive and pick someone out of the crowd. He's stiff-legged and keeps jerking his head as if he doesn't know where he is.

I walk back down the hallway, along the dark edge of sleeplessness. I'm losing something. I'm as empty as the night would be without the police lights, the helicopter, the dog barking.

I slip out the back door into the dark secrecy of the parking lot. The night air is as warm and digestible as the breath of moths. Desires erupt like stars. A current of wistfulness drifts through the darkness. The moon looks like a clock.

I go back in and lie down on my bed; the hours speed along my vertebrae—three o'clock, four o'clock, five. I think of the terrifying look in Dolores's eyes.

At five-thirty Gigi's lover slams his car door and drives away. I picture Gigi fluttering from her bed, the disarray of her bedclothes.

The morning is sharp and cool. It smells of weeds.

3

Web Desiderio

Web's nowhere in sight when I get off the plane at La Guardia Saturday morning. I head for the baggage claim with my carry-on bag in my arms like a baby. I'm getting dizzy watching the baggage conveyor belt when Web comes up behind me and starts twirling my hair.

"Did you join the Mile-High Club?" he says.

"What's that?"

"Doing it with someone in the plane restroom while you're in the air."

"Hello, Web," I say.

"You have to carry your own luggage because I got a crick in my back from croquet."

Web's short, musclebound, a pretty-boy who looks like trouble. He's cherubic with damp black eyes, curlicues of his jet black hair swirling out of his head like horns. You'd think he has a foreign accent from his dark, exotic face, but he sounds boys' prep. He's twenty-eight, three years younger than I, but in him I've discovered the Fountain of Immaturity. He's fourth-generation Princeton, but he doesn't get to move out of his slot until he has a scion of his own, which may be never.

Web is impeccably dressed in navy blue blazer, gray flannels, red and navy repp tie. He wears this straight look as a cover. I look down and see my reflection in his shoes.

"Where did your ancestors come from?" I ask him. Since I date Web only between his cruises like this, a lot of basic information falls through the cracks. "What sort of name is Web Desiderio?"

"Greenwich, Connecticut," he says. "There were seven Webs in my first grade."

"I mean, of what descent are you? From what part of the world?"

"What difference does it make?" he says. "You hate geography."

It's true. All I learned in parochial-school Geography was where the pagan babies came from and that coffee beans came from Brazil. Web dashes out, then pulls up a few minutes later in a red Ferrari. He buys a new car every year; it's his concrete manifestation of some new intrapsychic event.

"Don't *touch* me," he says, squeezing himself up against the car door as he drives out of the airport.

I laugh, then he dozes off at the wheel for a few seconds. He knows it scares me to death.

"Web!"

"I was just resting my eyes," he says.

"You were *asleep!*"

"Let's have a fight," he says.

"Let's have some tea," I say, reaching into the glove compartment for his Thermos, and I open the bag of cookies.

"When you eat a cookie you get this desperate look on your face," he says. "As if it's the only cookie in the world, the last one you'll ever eat."

"It may be, if you get us killed falling asleep at the wheel."

"No, really," he says. "When you crunch on that cookie you

get a wild look in your eye. When are we going to get married?"

"You know, I like a man with a good car."

He asks me three more times as we drive across the Triboro Bridge. He loves to ask and I love to say no. He'd be really upset if I said yes.

"You're a hard person to sell," he says. "Marriage, anything."

"It's because I don't *want* anything," I say.

We stop for lunch at Peter Rabbit's Salad Bar.

"Please can we lock the car?" I say.

"Nobody's going to steal your luggage."

We always go through this. My luggage has never been stolen but Web is always losing things. He leaves his wallet on the dashboard until someone steals it. When he was dressed up as Cupid for a Heart Association Valentine benefit, he left one arm of his expensive blue blazer hanging out of his car trunk and someone broke into it with his arrow. "CUPID ROBBED!" the newspaper headline said.

He won't lock the car, so I drag my luggage into the restaurant. He sighs, but one of the reasons he loves me is I'm so insecure.

"I'll watch your stuff while you go to the salad bar," he says.

I'm so struck by this kindness that at the salad bar I actually think about marrying him. Actually, he'd accept just about any partnership I'd consent to. I could live at his docko-minium while he's on his cruises and go off whenever I wanted to. He'd like the arrangement because he wants the latitude to mix business and pleasure.

"I'm being sexually harassed by my broker," he says when I come back with my salad. "She expects me to sleep with her in return for hot tips."

"How hot *are* her tips?" I say, repressing my jealousy.

"Why don't you rescue me?" he says.

"Isn't my being on retainer enough? At least my visits keep her from getting overly optimistic."

"But a broker should be optimistic."

"But not overly."

"If only she were married, she'd turn me on more," he says. "Married women are safe. Their husbands neglect them so they appreciate whatever attention I give them, but they're not trying to marry me by the third date. Single girls are desperate. 'I can't waste any more time on you if you're not serious,' they say."

"But Web, you give mixed messages. You're so attentive to a woman the second you meet her. She mistakes that for real interest."

"You knew I wasn't really interested in you," he says.

"I'm special because I have practically no self-esteem."

Web is Mr. Wrong; he loves me and I love him but only as far as we're able.

"Why can't we just have a normal, dull sex life like everyone else?" I say.

He doesn't answer; he nibbles at my salad. He won't get one of his own. He orders only off the menu, and there's no menu to order off here.

Web's dockominium in Norwalk, Connecticut is architecturally high-tech but furnished in old money. I've seen it before, but it always dazes me. "Where did you get all these eighteenth-century antiques?" I say, gazing at his marble statuary, burnished wood secretaries and hautboys, velvet settees, silver tea services.

"They've been in the family," he says.

I lived with Web once for two weeks, and by the time I left I felt that I, too, was museum-quality. I grew old, waiting for him to come home from dates with people's wives. Still,

I like knowing that Web appreciates fine things. I'm tiptoeing across the plush oriental when the phone rings. It sounds as if it must be one of his Top Wives, but he makes it quick.

"I'm not accepting any more calls," he says when he hangs up.

"You had a winner?"

"I love rich, married women," he says. "Let their husbands pay for the Rolex watches; all they want from me is a little attention. Are you with me on that?"

I just look at him.

"This one is stopping by after dinner," he says.

"But *I'm* your date," I protest. "I flew in for you."

"It's okay, she's bringing her husband," he says. "She wants to meet you."

"She wants to meet *me?*" I say. "Well, I don't want to meet *her.*"

"They're just coming by for a drink," he says, and puts eight bottles of Dom Pérignon into the refrigerator behind the bar.

"Two bottles each?" I say.

Web spends the afternoon cooking me a gourmet dinner, while I work on my new grant proposal for expanded prison library service. My mother cooked dinner while I did my homework. Although Web is trying to help me make myself as different from my mother as possible, sometimes he himself reminds me of her. But which one, the mother of my childhood or of my adolescence? At first, she was thin and tall, her shoulders pulled up in the forties style. Was that fashion, or to ward off my father's blows? Slouching was the fashion then, she scooped her breasts into her bra, but women's breasts are different now. When I grew into my teens, her height cascaded down over her body, padding her arms, her hips.

"Is this just a phase?" my mother asked when I sulked and refused to eat anything for breakfast but grapefruit sections.

"I hope this is just a phase," she said when my brother Doug spent hours in his room lighting matches. Just as her fear was growing milder, when we got away from our father, Doug and I sprouted into adolescent crankiness. We gave her new things to worry about.

Sometimes I think about all the things she taught me—how to pin clothes on the line, overlapping the edges of two sheets to make the clothespins go further. How much water to boil for the spaghetti and when to put the salt in, how to break the spaghetti to fit in the pot. I feel disloyal to her now when I soften an unbroken handful of pasta, when I tear romaine instead of cutting iceberg with a knife.

I can't concentrate on my grant proposal. I go fizz in Web's Jacuzzi, blow-dry my hair, play with my makeup. I slip on the seductive black lace lingerie Web gave me as a present, then hide it under my demure black silk dress.

Web serves our intimate little dinner by candlelight—fresh salmon mousse with shrimp and scallops lathered with green mayonnaise, salade Niçoise, veal *médaillons* with a cream mushroom and cognac sauce. By the time I remember I'm a vegetarian, we're on the chocolate truffle cake and it's too late.

"We have to be very careful," Web says. "The people coming tonight think I'm a Republican."

"What are you?" I say.

"A Libertine," he says in his conspiratorial whisper.

Web's paramour Gillian and her husband, Foster, arrive after dinner. I'm shocked to see they belong to our parents' generation. Gillian is a tall, ash-blond anorexic, but very well-preserved. Foster puffs like a blowfish. I get the definite impression they've come so Foster can see if the right sort of man is screwing his wife. Foster's a Princeton man, too, so it appears that everything is all right. I'm in a bit of a daze from Web's rich French food and the Dom Pérignon. Not much that Foster,

Gillian, or Web says makes any sense to me. It sounds like a mix of sexual innuendo and international economics. Everything is "terribly" this and "ghastly" that.

"Don't you think it's just *ghaaastly?*" Gillian says cozily to me.

"Oh, yes, I do," I say.

Web plays big-band music on his CD. The three of them dance; it turns out they're all expert ballroom dancers. During the conversation step, they talk only of its intricacies.

My mother scraped together money to send my brother Doug and me to ballroom dance lessons when I was thirteen. "I want you kids to be able to take care of yourselves," she said, and somehow that began with ballroom dancing, as if that were the real beginning of the life she wanted for us. I could learn the steps, but no one asked me to dance. The girls who were asked to dance were saucy, more developed, girls who giggled, and after the class I ran out the door and burst into tears in my mother's car. At home, she practiced the dance steps with Doug, the box step with "Moon River" on the record player.

It's as if, through his older friends and their entertainments, Web is trying to relive *his* life with his parents. His mother is dead, and he never talks about his father, but I get the feeling he loved them. It must be fun, being a scion. Web and Foster take turns doing the fox trot, the mambo, the tango with Gillian. I feel left out, but can't decide whether that's desirable or not. Web keeps pouring me Dom Pérignon. The pitch of the evening rises higher.

"What's *your* favorite dance, Colleen?" Gillian says to me.

"Aerobic," I say.

"Isn't she precious?" Gillian says to Foster.

"Show us!" Web says exuberantly, taking off the Lester Lanin and putting on a disco tape. This is why he's a good social director. I feel better when the music hits, my body responding to the beat with the freestyle disco moves and hip-hop street jazz Suzi is teaching us now for aerobic routines.

"Beautiful, beautiful!" Foster says, flushing with excitement.

I begin to see why Web loves this quasi-parental approval. It's as if they're approving of who he really is instead of just a scion. For me, it's like being noticed by my parents in the first place. I'm not sure they knew I was really there.

Web dances around me, tantalizingly lifts the edge of my silk dress. I'd forgotten I'm wearing such sexy lingerie. Foster has a fit of pleasure; Gillian glows at his excitement. I begin to feel like one of those girls they could get through the Personals to perk up their sex life.

"Gorgeous!" Foster whoops. Pushing himself up from the velvet sofa, he launches his bulk in my direction. He strips himself of his tie while doing a hula around me.

I undulate out of his grasp. It would be funny except that his face is so red he reminds me of one of those politicians who ruins his career by dying in flagrante delicto. The cover-up will fail and I'll have to go on talk shows to try to explain myself and it will be horrible. I look to Web for help.

Web lifts my dress over my head instead. I forget to be horrified in my champagne haze—it's all in fun, after all. I dance as if I've been let out of a cage. My aerobic steps benefit from a little more tits and ass. I'd be dangerous if I wore tassels. If I danced like this in aerobics, I'd have the lawyers and accountants at my feet.

Web looks as if he can't wait to make love to me tonight. Gillian lifts her pale hand, heavy with rings, and places it over her heart. Foster, however, looks as if he's about to come. Exploding with lust, he fumbles unsuccessfully with his buttons. He rips open his shirt. Buttons fly everywhere. Barrel chested and hairy, he looks like a fat Superman of Wall Street.

With the presence of mind that women who orchestrate affairs have to have, Gillian pulls Foster out the door. She blows kisses at Web and me all the way.

Web rushes me into the bedroom; I land in his four-poster with a bounce. But it's no use; he still shuts his eyes and starts fucking away.

"Haven't you even heard of foreplay?" I say.

"Ugh, please," he says. "Don't ruin everything!"

"I'm not attacking your manhood," I say. "I just want us to make love *together*."

He screws me through the hole in my crotchless panties, then he falls asleep at the wheel, just like in the car.

Most of the time I think my one true partner isn't even on the planet. I no longer deserve to find happiness in love because of the defilements with Web. I'm imprisoned and can get out only by some violent act against myself. If I were a planet, I'd blow myself up.

Web's a rogue, the real thing. Maybe I do outrageous things with him because I'm trying to understand the nature of evil. We're not really evil, just products of repressive up-bringings we misinterpreted to horrible effect. Our parochial-school nuns convinced us that the Sixth Commandment, "Thou shalt not commit adultery," literally applied to us. Web once told me that in spite of being an altar boy, he felt like a walking impure thought. I'm a Born-Again Pagan, and Web still goes to Mass on Sundays and Holy Days of Obligation, but sometimes I think we're trying to find out just how conditional God's love is.

I watch Web sleep. Web of the velvet dinner jacket and pink cummerbund, the Prince Charming escort service.

Where did my father's violence come from? Where did it go? I wanted to ask my mother: Was he charming up to the second drink, the third, and where did he go from there? Did he crank up, turn mean slowly, or did he just explode like the first firecracker on the Fourth of July? What did he give up when he gave up drinking? He seems to me like a man flaccid, depotentiated.

Because we children existed, my mother couldn't be happy. If it weren't for us, she could have been rid of my father and fallen in love and married someone else. The man would have taken good care of her and taken her to places like Bermuda. She'd have worn pretty clothes.

Instead, she had to worry all the time about how to take care of everything by herself and how to work to make money to feed us and to buy our coats and boots and to give us milk money for school. She never had time to herself because as soon as she got home from work she had to start cooking supper and listen to us at the same time. If we weren't there, supper wouldn't have been split three ways and she wouldn't have been so thin. After supper, she could have had coffee and a cigarette with a man instead of listening to us fight over TV. In the evening, she could have gone out dancing instead of helping us cover our school books with brown paper or washing our hair. If we weren't there, we wouldn't have kept coming up with new problems like cooties or the Asian flu or the holes in Dougie's new pants. He fell down every time he wore new pants to school, and I worried my mother to death with all my nervous habits, like pulling up my socks and picking where there was nothing to pick at. I switched to twirling my hair the way she did, but it didn't help. I drove her crazy asking her what if this happens or what if that happens. "I don't know dear, I don't know dear, I don't know," she shouted at me when I pushed her past her limit. When I told her I'd babysit Doug if she went out on a date, she said "What, do you want me to be like Mrs. Scully?" Mrs. Scully went out with men she met where she was a waitress, and her son became a juvenile delinquent.

My mother's eyes teared when she laughed. She wiped at the corners of her eyes with the hankie she kept up her sleeve.

When my father still lived with us, when he and she got dressed up and had company and served drinks and canapés, my mother got me out of bed to cry for the company. I could cry at will; my record was three seconds. "Watch this," she'd say to the guests, then she'd hold up her watch and say "Go!" I don't remember what I thought about; after a while it didn't matter.

I wake up the next morning with Web leaning over me. "Today's the New York Marathon," he says. "Get up."

He's already dressed in his running shorts and shoes. I'm still undressed in the remnants of last night's dishabille. I pull the pillow over my head.

"You may not run with your Walkman," he says.

"I can't run without it. Besides, what could we talk about for six hours?"

"It's not going to take us six hours."

"Yes it will," I say.

So many people are running this marathon that we have to park in Brooklyn, then run back across the Verrazano-Narrows Bridge to the starting line. By then the race has started and everyone else is gone.

"I hate it already," I tell him.

"I'll commit to running the entire way with you, slow as you are, if you'll commit to finishing."

"That's very nice," I say. "If I hate it now, how deeply am I going to hate it at the twenty-sixth mile?"

"You always say I won't commit," he says. "A hundred

thousand American men are hearing that this minute and every minute."

"I always say you ought to be *committed*," I say, turning up my Walkman.

A few straggling spectators look up in surprise as we run by. "Everyone else went by a long time ago," one of them says.

"I didn't really train for this, you know," I tell Web. "Unless you count aerobic dancing as cross-training."

"Is that like cross-dressing?" he says.

My legs stay cold all through Brooklyn because we forgot to do warm-up stretches; we just started running like a couple of fools. "Let's hold hands," I say.

"We can't run holding hands."

"You have a fear of intimacy," I say.

I keep switching channels on my Walkman because I can't stand to run to commercials. Web loves commercials; he always turns them up on his radio. I love classical music, but I can't stand to run to it, and I can't run to Spanish stations either. I like to run in my own language.

We have a head wind the whole time we're running in Brooklyn. I put on one glove discarded by a warmed-up runner far ahead of us. Web spots the other glove a few hundred yards later and offers it to me.

"You wear it," I say.

We run like that, each with a glove on our inside hand.

"What do you love about me?" I ask him.

"I *understand* you," he says, pulling a Kleenex out of his sock to blow his nose.

I love that he keeps a Kleenex in his sock; it's one of the things I know about him that no one else knows.

"Do you think I'm beautiful?" I say.

"You're cute," he says.

"I don't want to be cute, I want to be beautiful."

"No, really," he says, "some men like cute girls."

Ahead of us are three girls who are beautiful, not cute. Web runs as if he's trying to catch up with them. I'm torn between trying to keep up with him and slowing down to keep him with me.

In Queens we run past a water station. We each grab a cup with our outside hand and keep running. We gulp down the water and drop our cups; it's one of the few times in life you're supposed to litter.

"I hope no one from Houston sees me taking six hours to run a marathon," I say.

"I wish they could have seen you last night," he says.

I wince. "I'd lose my library job. You don't have to work, so you don't understand. You could just stay home and man-age your portfolio."

"I don't manage my portfolio, I manage the management of my portfolio," he says.

"I've never understood why you're a cruise-ship social direc-tor when you don't have to work," I say.

"I like the milieu," he says. "Lots of lonely women with beautiful manners."

"But ship's policy prohibits your having relationships with them," I say, feeling another stab of jealousy.

"I don't have relationships, only romances," he says. "When they've had a few drinks they think I'm a social *worker* and tell me everything. Sometimes I even get a little action."

"How do you get away with it?" I demand.

"Everyone wants to feel special," he says.

I run and wonder why Dolores is in jail, and why I find Web lovable in spite of the things he does and makes me do. He looks at me and I look at him; he reminds me of one of those starving children you can help or turn the page. That's how he looked when I first saw him, being auctioned off as

Most Eligible Bachelor. It wasn't until several dates into our relationship that I realized he had a problem with intimacy. It's as if he's stuck in quicksand and the only way I can help him is to get in the quicksand myself. Is that why I did what I did last night? I tried to maintain a certain detachment while trying to get off on whatever pleasure there was to be had.

"Most people think about dropping out at the sixteenth mile," he says, and he's right, but he talks me through it as we're running across the Fifty-ninth Street Bridge.

We pass a supine woman being worked on by paramedics.

"She'll get the Best Jewelry Award," Web says.

"That's more than I'll get," I say.

"You'll get Best Makeup," he says.

"Where's this wall everyone talks about hitting?" I say at the twentieth mile, but at the twenty-first I hit it. I start to cry.

He's hurting too; I can see it when we look into each other's eyes. He looks worried; he takes another Kleenex out of his sock and wipes the tears off my face. We're running more slowly than walking. Two race officials head in our direction.

"Don't lean on me," Web says. "They'll make you drop out if they know you're in trouble."

I straighten up. It doesn't hurt so much because I can't feel my legs anymore.

"We're okay," he says.

By the twenty-third mile I want to die.

My heart beating out of my chest, I feel my father's fists beat my mother's white body, spotting it with bruises as purple and yellow as pansies. I came out of her thin, white body. I feel the desire to hit rise and rise like sexual tension. I'm desperate to separate myself from them—my mother and father—from my desire for them and theirs for me.

He beats her as if he's beating at her door, he beats at the door of her. As if she's his mother, refusing to give him her breast, refusing to give herself to him. But my mother gives herself up to his fists, she offers her body to him so he can enter her this way. So that he'll no longer be outside of her, beating her, the white softness of her thin body, spotted yellow and purple.

I'm afraid of my anger, afraid of my own desire. This is how I feel both anger and desire. Like Web, banging away at my sex. The two of us—him banging, and me crying to get in.

By the time we cross the finish line in Central Park, all the spectators have gone. All the prizes have been awarded.

"We did it!" Web says.

"Thanks for helping me finish," I say.

"I *know* you," he says. "I know the difference in your tears between real pain and just crying."

4

The Emergency Room

When I come home from my weekend with Web, Mrs. Fritz is sitting with St. Francis at his kitchen table. The mom and pop of the Lord's Motel, they're like the woodcutter and his wife in a fairy tale. Gigi, Barbara, and I could be their three daughters—Gigi the pretty one, Barbara the clever one, and I the devoted one who will tend the fire and stir the soup until they grow old and die.

"You haven't made peace with the *Lord?*" St. Francis shouts at Mrs. Fritz in horror.

They appear to be in the middle of a row about religious beliefs. Of course, Mrs. Fritz's hearing is so poor that an ordinary conversation sounds like a fight. St. Francis believes fanatically in everything from Baptist fundamentalism to New Age meditation and sees no contradictions among these. He's an indiscriminate synthesizer; Mrs. Fritz is an analyzer. She's critical of dogma of any kind, whether rigid or user-friendly.

"I haven't made peace with him and I haven't *not* made peace with him," Mrs. Fritz says. "What the heck difference does it make?"

St. Francis shuts his eyes tightly, as if praying for inner guidance. Mrs. Fritz winks at me.

In this lull between rounds, I remember how I loved to visit Mrs. Fritz with Service-to-the-Unserved. Her old house on lower Westheimer was furnished in old-lady antiques, green velvet chairs, ballerina figurines. Over this was a layer of modern civilization's flotsam and jetsam—junk mail, tiny cactuses in plastic pots, *TV Guides*. Lined up in a row on the back of her sofa were fifteen small stuffed animals, gifts from various outlived relatives. She told me which was from whom, until the teddy bears in ice skating skirts and pandas in tiny college T-shirts came to represent for me her dead relatives themselves. She camped out on one end of this sofa, everything in reach—box of tissues, tall stack of books, telephone, afghan, plastic Astros cup of iced tea. Her mind grew sharper as her body fell away, the skin collapsing fold by fold. She read prodigiously, every Large Print book the library had until she resorted to regular print with a magnifying glass. She pored over it like Sherlock Holmes, searching for new ideas.

"Then what's our purpose in life?" St. Francis shouts, finally opening his eyes.

"How should I know?" she says. "We search and we search and we don't get much for it." She looks triumphant, as if this is somehow an entirely satisfying conclusion to come to.

When I brought her books on lower Westheimer, she'd insist on getting up to fix me a cup of tea. I wanted to get it myself, but I didn't want to interfere with her autonomy. I'd offer her my arm, and we'd reel together from the living room to her kitchen. A huge set of wind chimes hung from the ceiling, and she invariably crashed into it on her way into the kitchen. It sounded as if the entire percussion section at the symphony had fallen off the stage. I worried about her as she lit the gas burner with shaking hands, poured the boiling water into our teacups. "Have you ever thought of moving into a nice retirement home?" I asked her. "Give me a break, dearie," she said. "What would I have in common with old people?"

St. Francis still looks nonplussed when Barbara walks in with Gigi. We make room for them at the kitchen table. Already gaining weight from the baby, Barbara gets the outside chair; her days of sliding into the one next to the wall are over.

"Did you have all your doodads checked?" Mrs. Fritz asks her.

"Doodads?" Barbara says.

"Your chromosomes, dearie," Mrs. Fritz says.

"I don't need amniocentesis," Barbara says. "My chromosomes are fine."

"It's the welder's we're worried about," Gigi says.

Barbara gazes coolly at her with eyes as blue as the big Texas sky. St. Francis's phone rings. Maybe it's the welder with his retort. St. Francis can't answer it because he's up to his elbows in carrots for Gigi's and Barbara's juice. Mrs. Fritz is closest to the phone so she picks it up.

"What?" she hollers into the receiver. "Whaaaat, I can't hear you!"

Barbara, Gigi, and I discuss Barbara's pregnancy while St. Francis rinses the juicer. He's probably trying to come up with one final New Age Texan apologia that will turn Mrs. Fritz into a believer of some sort.

"It was an obscene caller," Mrs. Fritz huffs when she hangs up several minutes later. "I had to keep asking him to speak up."

"I love it," Gigi says. "It serves him right."

Then Mrs. Fritz faints in a heap. She has never done that before. We all freeze for one horrible moment. My voice quivering, I call 911 while Barbara tries to find Mrs. Fritz's pulse. Gigi runs outside to wait for the ambulance. St. Francis tears apart his cabinets looking for medicinal white willow bark.

Did the obscene phone call make Mrs. Fritz faint? Is it temporary indignation or a heart attack? What if she's dying?

The ambulance arrives with lights and sirens. The paramedics rush in, Gigi leading them like a SWAT team. They put a plastic oxygen tube to Mrs. Fritz's mouth, an I.V. in her arm, attach electrocardiogram patches to her chest. They wrap her in a blanket and load her onto a collapsible gurney, roll her out the door. Terrified, I go with her in the ambulance, hanging on for dear life.

They back up the ambulance to the emergency room. I run to keep up with the gurney. Two people converge on it at once—a peevish admissions clerk with a clipboard, and the emergency room doctor, his starched white coat embroidered with *Gabriel Benedict, M.D.* in royal blue script.

"Does the patient have insurance?" the clerk demands.

"I think so," I say.

"What's the policy number?" she says.

"I don't know," I say, panicking.

The clerk looks ready to push Mrs. Fritz back out the door.

Dr. Benedict looks into my eyes. "She has insurance," he says firmly to the clerk, elbowing her out of the way. "Let's get a CBC, PT, PTT, full set of chemistries, glucose, and arterial blood gas, please," he says to the nurse. "Also an EKG and a chest x-ray."

I'm at a loss to answer Dr. Benedict's questions about Mrs. Fritz's medical history. I'm relieved to see her transferred from the ambulance's collapsible gurney onto the hospital's sturdier one. Dr. Benedict and I hover together over her until he sends me out to the waiting room.

"I'll let you know as soon as I get the results from her tests," he says.

In the waiting room, I anxiously study the beige walls, the linoleum floor, the ceiling's acoustic tile. This is a room where people try not to go crazy with fear. They hold the parts of themselves that hurt—heads, stomachs. They're wrapped in homemade bandages; a workman's hand bleeds through paper towels. A small, frightened girl sits by the door, head in her hand, her elbow leaning on one knee. Who's she waiting for, gazing down the hall toward the treatment rooms?

Gigi arrives and slides into a molded vinyl chair next to mine. "How is she?" she says.

"I don't know," I say, wringing my hands. "Oh, Gigi, I didn't even know what to tell the doctor about her medical history."

"Mrs. Fritz isn't the type to talk about her ailments," she says. "It's not your fault."

"She has no sense of balance, her hearing is terrible, her skin is falling off her bones," I say. "What if that all *means* something?"

"It means she's *old*," Gigi says.

"Just because she's old doesn't mean there's not a *reason*," I say. But I know Gigi doesn't mean that. Still, when someone makes it to ninety-five it's as if she has earned some favored status. "I know it's crazy," I say, "but I think if Mrs. Fritz can make it to one hundred then she won't die at all."

"You're right, it's crazy," Gigi says. "Speaking of crazy, how was your weekend with Web?"

The waiting room buzzes with an anxious undertone. Women hold whimpering babies in their laps, children look aged by whatever disaster they've seen. I listen to snatches of conversation: "...Why are you so stupid?...What you say?...She's in fair condition, can't see her...chest pains now?" A policeman describes a traffic fatality to the victim's family.

"It was insane," I say. "I keep thinking that if I could break Web of the weird parts of our relationship, we'd be free to enjoy the good parts. He's actually very funny and smart and entertaining the rest of the time."

"It doesn't work that way," she says. "Now that you've established that kinky pattern, you'll never break him of it."

"If only I could find the key to his psyche," I say. "If only I could get through to his real feelings."

"Those *are* his real feelings," she explodes. "He's *kinky*. He's destroying your psyche while you're looking for the key to his."

I hunch my shoulders and look around to see if everyone heard her. "This is not the place to talk about this," I say. It's ridiculous to be agonizing over Web when Mrs. Fritz is so ill.

"Sorry," she says, lowering her voice and patting my arm. "We're both upset about Mrs. Fritz. Did you and Web do anything normal?"

"We ran the New York Marathon, but it was like running alongside Web while he chased other women," I say. "Isn't there anyone in between the seminarians I dated in high school who refused to hold my hand and this kinky screwball? Where are all the red-blooded American boys I was promised for my virtue?"

"Killed in Vietnam or gay," she says.

Ultraviolet lights to kill germs cast a blue glow. The air conditioning is too cold; a woman dozes under a shroudlike sheet. A crack addict in a black T-shirt that reads "Satan kissed my dog" sidles around the edges of the room. An old man paces back and forth, carrying his urine in a plastic bag.

"But where was I when the live straight ones were getting married?" I say.

"They got married to all the cheerleaders when you weren't looking."

"Like my sister-in-law, Miss Teenage Massachusetts," I say. "And you, even if you had to throw him back."

Gigi laughs at this reference to Henry as a fish. He's history, and now she's crazy about a man she sells software with. Gigi and Jack want to get married, sometimes even to each other, but never at the same time.

"*Jack* is great in bed," she says. She says his name as if she's delighted with him for having such a name and with herself for finding a man with so wonderful a name as Jack. "He's been engaged twice, but never married. Plus, he makes a wonderful presentation."

"Sales presentation?" I say.

"I mean he's a sharp dresser, Colleen," she says, making a face at me. "Although he also sold the most software in our regional division."

"That's really terrific," I say. I feel awful. If I'd been married and divorced like Gigi, it'd be years before I met someone else. I seem to suffer major karmic consequences for everything, while everyone else gets off scot-free. Very much like Saturday Confession years ago, when I got a long list of prayers to say for penance for my relatively short list of venial sins. I knelt at the altar, flickering like a votive candle, long after the other kids had bicycled home.

"I'm not trying to make you feel worse, I'm just trying to tell you there are good men like Jack out there," she says.

I try not to hate Gigi. It's not her fault she's attractive to men. At parties, she's surrounded by four of them with two others circling, looking for an opening. She doesn't have to work the crowd; the crowd works her. "I wish *I* could meet a man at work," I say.

"Aren't there any single male librarians?" she says.

"Not straight ones," I say. "Of course, they're all very nice and they make good presentations."

"Maybe you should change careers," she says.

By now I've bitten off every one of my nails and am frantic

about Mrs. Fritz. I wish I'd brought a book so I wouldn't have to talk to Gigi. There's nothing to read in the waiting room but newspaper parts under chairs. And signs, like the bilingual one that reads "If you have been waiting in the emergency waiting room for more than six hours, please notify the charge nurse." A Hispanic woman studies it, rocking back and forth.

Finally Dr. Benedict appears in the doorway of the waiting room and motions us into the hall. He's lean, tall as an archangel, with a thick shock of hair so blond it's almost white. It's nearly midnight, and his five o'clock shadow has a head start on his square chin. He looks about thirty-five. He wears a navy blue tie printed with discreet white whales. Fluorescent light glints off his wedding ring as he waves his hand in the air to tell us about Mrs. Fritz.

"All her tests came back negative," he says. "She has a normal electrocardiogram, no chest pains, she's alert and clear-headed and shows no signs of head injury."

"What happened to her, then?" I say.

"She had a syncopal episode of unknown etiology," he says.

"She fainted and you don't know why," Gigi says.

"Yes," he says. "But she came through it."

He and I meet each other's gaze. The deep blue of his eyes is as clear as the night sky. His intelligence is palpable, electrifying. He burns so intensely with kindness that I feel penetrated by it. This man loves me and I love him, I think. I almost faint except that since he's married, I've already put him out of my mind.

He walks back down the hall to retrieve Mrs. Fritz as if he has slain a minor dragon. The totality of him is so wonderful I can't relate to it in any one part of myself. "He's the most gorgeous man I've ever seen," I say when I catch my breath.

"He looks like a lifeguard," Gigi says.

"He does not," I say. "He looks more ... academic than that."

"He has a swimmer's bones," she says.

"That's not the same as a lifeguard," I say. Gigi and I are already fighting over him, although he's married and Gigi already has a man. "At least we both agree he's gorgeous."

"Of course we think he's gorgeous," she snips. "He probably saved Mrs. Fritz's life."

Gigi and I take Mrs. Fritz home in Gigi's BMW. I help Mrs. Fritz get settled for the night. I fuss over her; I want her to get some sleep but I'm afraid to leave her alone. She's convinced the obscene phone call made her faint and that it won't happen again. I try to find out whether she has fainted before, but she has something else on her mind.

"Let me tell you something, dearie," she says, her hair even whiter against the pillow. "Lying on that hospital table? I floated straight up to the ceiling. Love glided in, like a piece of sky. I looked down and saw myself as an ancient queen."

"You had a near-death experience?" I say incredulously.

"What?" she says.

"A *near-death* experience?" I shout, hoping no one else hears me.

"Light pierced my lucid tissue, my inside self glowed dense as rubies," she goes on. "I was restored after waging peace in a difficult land. When I succumbed to the kindness of you and that doctor, I knew who I am and why I'm here."

"Why *are* we here?" I say.

"Love," she says.

"Because of love or to love other people?" I shout.

She doesn't answer; she seems even more hard of hearing than before.

"One other thing, dearie," she says, taking my hand. "Looking down, I saw you and that doctor in some kind of holy relationship."

"What do you mean?" I say, but she drifts off, smiling beatifically.

That night, untroubled by dreams of Web, I fall asleep to the sea-sounds of traffic from the Southwest Freeway.

5

Killer Bees

The next morning I wash my breakfast dishes and leave for the office at seven-forty-five. I stop at the gas station on my way to work.

"Please check the tires to be at least thirty-two but not more than thirty-four," I say, "and fill it up with regular." When I got my Master's in Library Science I bought myself a black boa and started going to Full Serve.

Transvestites are picking up coffee at the Stop N Go. Other people are waiting at bus stops. I stop at a red light. I like to notice everything, watch everyone, but you have to do it while staring straight ahead and looking confident and pleasant. A man pushing a shopping cart of crushed aluminum cans stares into my front windshield, at my office face and my office clothes.

"I wouldn't want an inside job," he says.

I have the disconcerting feeling that these are all moving parts of myself.

I drive through the Fourth Ward—a Southern city ghetto, everyone out on his porch at eight in the morning. I don't understand it. Today they're warming their hands over a barrel turned on its side, flames leaping out. Are they roasting chestnuts? If my car breaks down, will they attack me, help me, ignore me?

I like to be at the library by eight, to be a good example to myself. Sometimes I can't get out of bed on time. Then I'm behind all day, trailing guilt like a bridal veil.

I get coffee from the machine in the staff lounge, even though its water is suspect. You never know if this is the day it's taking two dimes and one nickel or five nickels or one quarter or three nickels and one dime for half a Styrofoam cup of brown water teeming with old coffee-machine microbes. Usually there aren't any cups left and you have to ask the secretaries where they're hiding them.

"There's not enough money in the budget to waste these," Lucille says, grudgingly handing me a cup.

Lucille, the secretary in charge of pouring the water into the coffee maker, lies down a lot on the vinyl sofa in the Ladies Room. She walks as if she's wearing bedroom slippers, the way women who have both foot and gynecological problems do. I never lie down in the ladies room because I can't stand to have a steady stream of people ask if I'm having cramps when it's only angst.

I go back to my office with the poisoned coffee and study my war map. A red pushpin for the jail, blue pins for nursing homes, and yellow pins for homebound individuals. I'm gazing at it, empire-building, when my boss Joanne buzzes me.

"Colleen, the Public Relations Team tells me you refuse to publicly relate with them," she says.

"They think Service-to-the-Unserved should conform to what they say about it instead of vice versa," I say.

"Honey, let me tell you something," she says. "What people think you're doing is always more important than what you're doing. Are you going to keep the public trust or go work at a branch?"

"I'll pencil in the Public Relations Team for a year from now," I promise.

"And now go talk to Ralph," she says. "The Bookmobile feels threatened."

Ralph, the Bookmobile librarian, feels his empire eroding, and every full moon he has a crisis about it.

"Ralph," I say when I buzz him. "Pencil me in, I'm on my way down."

When I get to the Bookmobile office, Ralph is perched on the edge of his chair. He has hemorrhoids.

"For your birthday," I say, "I'm going to give you one of those doughnut cushions to sit on."

"You're gobbling up all the state money," he says. He must have gotten wind of my new grant proposal.

"We're serving different populations. None of my Unserved can come out and get on your Bookmobile."

"But we're Outreach too."

"Service-to-the-Unserved is a further reach of Outreach."

"They took the jail away from me and gave it to you," he says.

"Your suburbs are nicer," I say.

"They don't need me in the suburbs anymore either," he says dolefully. "Between the proliferation of branch libraries and Books-by-Mail, I'm being squeezed out. Now you and Service-to-the-Unloved, and that's it for me."

"I'm really sorry, Ralph," I say. Ralph and I are actually on the same side. The normal librarians regard outreach librarians as outlaws, and someone's always eyeing our projects for budget cuts.

"Mother always liked you best," he says.

"She's sending me to a branch if I don't make Service-to-the-

Unserved work," I say. "Or worse, to Technical Services to catalog for the rest of my life."

"But I heard that you cried your way through Cataloging and Classification in library school."

"I did," I say, remembering it with horror.

"I'm sorry to get on your case," Ralph says. "You can't imagine what it's like to drive the Bookmobile in Houston traffic."

"How do you do it?"

"Signal right, but turn left."

"Ralph!" I say.

I drive to the jail to discuss my new proposal for expanded library service with Lieutenant Sprunt, but he's already upset with me.

"Are you responsible for these books on the killer bees?" he says.

"Your residents requested them," I say.

"Stop calling them 'residents,' damn it," he says. "They're inmates to you—I won't tell you what *I* call them."

When I entered the jail, I felt the hum of excitement, very much like the buzzing of bees. I'm used to this; a good librarian picks up on current reading enthusiasms. Prisoners have fads like everyone else. Sometimes they're all reading machine-gun paperbacks, sometimes they all want to learn to play the guitar.

"I'm not bringing in any bees themselves, I'm providing books *about* the bees," I tell Lieutenant Sprunt.

"What do you know about these killer bees?" he says, as if I'm part of some conspiracy.

"The correct term is Africanized bees, and they're no different from other bees except they're more defensive and can sting more than once," I say.

Lieutenant Sprunt reads to me from a book on his desk:

" 'Africanized drone bees will mate with European queen bees. A queen bee lays thousands of eggs each day and so within two or three weeks a nest contains twenty to thirty *thousand* Africanized bees.' " He slams the book closed.

"That's a lot of bees," I say.

"How many of these killer bee books have you brought in here?" he says.

"I'll have to check the circulation statistics," I say. "I've exhausted the library's inventory and have had to order more on interlibrary loan."

"They're more aggressive, there are a lot more of them, they can sting more," he says, leaning back in his enormous chair.

"Do you suspect your residents—I mean the inmates—of breeding bees?" I say.

His chair springs forward with an alarming clang. His face and neck turn hot red, he belches at me in perfect exasperation. "Of course not!" he says. "Why don't you tell *me* why they've got this bug in their ear?"

"We all seek our affinities with nature," I say. "Some people watch birds, some people garden, and some people like killer bees."

"You liberal arts majors are all alike," he says.

"They're just learning something new," I say.

"That's what I'm afraid of," he says, standing up.

I think I see steam rising from the top of his sweating head. I hope he doesn't have a heart attack. I don't want to start over with someone new who hates jail library service even more. "I'm worried about you," I say. "I'm going to bring you everything the library has on relaxation techniques."

"I get every crazy off the street in here," he says. "Lawsuits for overcrowding, the state prison won't take the felons they're responsible for because *they're* overcrowded, the vegetarians are suing the kitchen."

"There, there," I say, humoring him.

He mops the top of his wet head, then rushes off to quell a riot somewhere.

Dolores is waiting for me in the jail lobby. She stands helplessly next to an empty book cart, while policemen, lawyers, guards, and escorted inmates rush past. Lieutenant Sprunt has authorized her to meet me here, but she looks uncomfortable, trapped between the jail world and the world outside. It would be impossible for Dolores to escape; the armed guards at the door look as if they'd shoot first, ask questions later. She reminds me of myself as a little girl, standing in the middle of a babysitter's kitchen after being dropped off from nursery school. I waited for hours for my mother to get off work and pick me up. The babysitter's family rushed by, busy with a life I wasn't part of. I was too frightened by my own family life to trust theirs, even for an afternoon.

The lobby is a cramped area with grimy gray walls, a gray concrete floor, excruciatingly bright fluorescent lighting. A pay phone hangs on a wall covered with scribbled numbers, between a cigarette machine and an empty candy machine.

"Hello, Dolores," I say, as cheerfully as possible. I dump my heavy canvas bag of library books on a long wooden bench.

"Mornin', ma'am," she says, sounding depressed and anxious.

I wonder if she's still apprehensive about doing this job. Really, I have no idea of her distribution problems inside the jail. "I'm supposed to tell you you can't have any more books on killer bees, but I can't do that," I say.

"Yes, ma'am," she says.

I help her load this month's library books onto her book cart. She puts the new books on bees back into my canvas bag. We look at one another.

"It ain't worth you getting in trouble, ma'am," she says.

"What else would the residents like to read?" I say.

"A few of them, anything you got. But most of them, they don't want to read nothing."

"That's because they weren't read to as children," I say, sounding dubious even to myself. "We need to spark their interest in books."

"Yes, ma'am," she says. "But a lot of them *can't* read."

"Not to worry," I say. "I'll write a literacy component into my new proposal."

"Yes, ma'am," she says.

"I'll need your help to enlist Lieutenant Sprunt's support."

"Yes, ma'am," she says.

"Please call me Colleen," I say. Her deference seems incongruous with the intelligence burning in her brown eyes. I want to know why she's in jail, but I'm afraid to ask. "What are your own reading interests?" I say instead.

"I don't have much time to read," she says.

"We need you to set a good example for the other residents," I say. "Didn't you say you were interested in art books?"

"Books on learning to draw," she says, hanging her head. "That was dumb."

"It's not a bit dumb," I say, but I feel how inconsequential one's interests could become here. Walking into the jail is like passing into the horrors of the daily news; my own concerns seem frivolous. Murder, rape, and robbery are in the air. It's all one can do to bear up under the madness of it. "Here, I brought you a few drawing books," I say, offering them to her.

She takes them as if they'll burn her fingers, then wraps her arms around them like a schoolgirl. "Thanks," she says.

"You're so welcome," I say. "I'll bring more the next time."

"Oh, no," she says, alarmed. "It's just, I got other things on my mind. I can't be goofing off."

"You're missing the whole point of rehabilitation, Dolores,"
I say. She looks at me as if I'm crazy, which of course is how
I sound. "Perhaps you have some vocational interests?"

She studies her nails. They're short and chipped, but clean.
"I didn't finish high school," she says. "But what I want to
be? Maybe I could be a manicurist. Or maybe I could fix hair."

At that moment, I want more than anything to fix Dolores.
Her entire demeanor is that of someone who wants to improve
herself, but doesn't know how. She speaks with the forced
grammar, slightly off, of someone who knows she's an unedu-
cated person speaking to an educated one. I want desperately
to help her get her life in order, get her G.E.D., vocational
training. I want to inspire her to take responsibility for herself,
get the legal help to leave this horrible, overcrowded jail.

"Dolores," I say. "Do you have a good attorney?"

"I got a court-appointed one," she says with a shrug. "He's
kind of busy."

"I'll bring you some law reference books," I say. "Can you
tell me what laws you're interested in?"

She looks blankly at me. She doesn't trust me, and why
should she? Do I imagine she'll say what crime she committed
and we'll go from there? *Vernon's Texas Codes Annotated,*
the statutes, definitions, historical notes, cross-references, law
review commentaries, and notes of decisions. I'm getting a
headache from my library-school memories of law books.

"I won't understand those books," she says, ashamed. "I
can read, but not that good."

"First things first, then," I say to reassure her. "I'll bring
you a dictionary and some appropriate texts so we can enhance
your reading skills." But how long will this take? How much
time has she got? What's time like for a prisoner, anyway?

She looks down at the floor. She's an island of passivity
in the chaotic frenzy of the lobby, guards and inmates rushing

by. I can bring her library materials, but I can't make her read. She's not stupid, but she's defeated. I'm overwhelmed by the enormity of Dolores's task, by the intensity of my need to help her. Each of her problems points to a deeper one. It's hard to know whether to start with her deepest feelings about herself and work outward, or with more superficial things and work in.

"So you'd like to be a manicurist?" I say, opting for the middle range. "Or you'd like to fix hair?" This is, after all, the kind of help she's asking for. My concern for her fights with my horror of being condescending.

"I want hair like yours," she says.

I want her to have counseling for her lack of self-esteem, get on an exercise program, spruce up her self-image. If I were her image consultant, I'd put her in a great short perm. Is her fashion personality a Natural or a Romantic? A Dramatic, maybe. No—a Classic. A designer suit, pearls, important earrings. My heart goes out to her—I wish I could give her a Day of Beauty at my salon. A scientific facial, pedicure, special occasion makeup, the works.

"I'll bring you some beauty-school vocational manuals the next time I come," I promise.

I could cry at the look of gratitude she gives me. I vow that when she gets out of jail, I'll give her a gift certificate from my salon for a Cut and Style with the Master Stylist.

6

The Living Bank

After work I'm going to a Unitarian meeting about organ donation. I've given up trying to meet men at gallery openings and cocktail parties. They're wall-to-wall with single women bumping into each other, stupefied that the few men there are too weird for words. I won't have to sparkle for the Unitarians, but I'd better get my nails done.

"Your nails are my children," Cleopatra, my manicurist, says.

She's making an example of me. In the window of her shop, called Nail Psychiatry, is an enormous black-and-white photo of my hands labeled "Before." "These are the worst nails I've ever seen," she said when I walked into her shop six months ago. I sat on my hands. "Get up off your hands, honey," she said, "we got work to do."

Cleopatra's a regal woman with rich black hair piled high on her head with gold combs. The shop is crowded with ladies getting nail wraps, pedicures.

"Why don't you work out of a big beauty salon?" I ask her.

"They're like HMOs where they rush you through from one doctor to another. When you got a problem like you got, you need to see a specialist."

"It's not my fault," I say.

"Of course it isn't, honey."

She slathers some kind of astringent from my wrists to my fingers and wipes it off like a mother washing a child's hands. I can't believe I spend money on manicures when children are starving in India. But taking care of my nails is a message of hope to my fingers that they'll one day get engaged.

"Did you read in the paper this morning 'bout that little boy snuck into the zoo at night and got eaten by a polar bear?" Cleopatra says, dunking one of my hands in soapy water. She scrubs my cuticles viciously.

"No," I say.

"I *cried*," she says. "Think of that little boy's mama. They shot that polar bear."

I'd cry for the bear. "If the kid broke into the zoo and was stupid enough to climb in with a polar bear he deserved to be eaten."

She slams my hand down on the towel. She's silent for several minutes, jabbing away with the orange stick and nail scissors. I've learned to always let the manicurist take the lead in conversation.

"How you get such weak nails?" she says finally.

"Maybe it's the Pill," I say.

"You married?"

"No." She knows I'm not married; she's just out for revenge because of the polar bear.

"You ever *been* married?"

"Never," I say. "Have you?"

"Twice," she says. "Leo women can get men but they can't keep them. I got an eight-hundred-dollar bed, though."

"What did you do with your engagement ring each time you got divorced?"

"Pawned it. If I had nails as weak as yours I'd go celibate."

She files my nails like a sad violinist. "What happened there?" she accuses, pointing at a ragged edge.

"I didn't start out to bite it; it broke half off and I had to bite off the rest."

"Mmmmmhmmmm, girl," she says.

"Do you think you'll ever get married again?"

"I'm too independent; men are afraid of an independent woman." She shakes the bottle of base coat. "That polar bear just ate that little boy *up*."

She applies the base, a special one for problem nails called Potion Z. I brace myself for the disagreement we have each week about nail polish.

"You don't need no polish," she says. "You need to give you nails a chance to breathe. This Potion Z is all you need, girl."

Some weeks she wins and some weeks I do. You can't even tell I've been for a manicure if I don't get colored polish. But today I'm unspeakably irritated at the stupidity of the boy who got eaten by the polar bear.

"I really would like some Pluperfect Pink," I press.

She sighs and applies the hot-pink polish. A man, obviously an admirer, taps on the window and waves at Cleopatra.

"That's a nice-looking man," I say.

"He ain't got nothin'," she says.

"What is it you're looking for him to have?"

"Money," she says, and grins at me.

I always ask for Pluperfect Pink because I have a bottle at home and can touch it up when it gets chipped. I sit with splayed fingers while it dries. She takes my money out of my purse so I won't screw up the polish.

Maybe Dolores could start out as a manicurist and wind up a businesswoman like Cleopatra. There's nothing wrong with being a manicurist; I don't feel sorry for Cleopatra. It's Cleopatra who feels sorry for *me,* for being a librarian.

•

I crash the Living Bank party. The hostess hugs me, the way Unitarians do, and fills out my name tag.

"I read about this in your newsletter," I apologize. I subscribe to the Unitarian newsletter because I'm fascinated by the way they believe in everything.

"Have you given much thought to whether you'd like coffee or champagne?" she asks. "It's completely up to you, and if you don't want either, that's okay too."

"I'd like both, please," I say.

I sit down on the floor in front of the coffee table. Everybody's eating Pepperidge Farm cookies and signing as witnesses on each other's Living Bank forms. A doctor and a lawyer are arguing about whether the Directive to Physicians form against prolonging life by artificial means means that the body can't be kept alive long enough to get the Living Bank organs out in decent shape. I think about putting some cookies in my pocket but decide that might seem like theft even to Unitarians.

"Would you sign as one of my witnesses?" I say to a tall man with his back toward me who reminds me of Dr. Gabriel Benedict.

"It'd be a pleasure," he says, turning around.

I'm shocked to my toes to see he really *is* Dr. Benedict. "Thank you," I say when I recover my voice. "Thank you for taking such good care of Mrs. Fritz in the emergency room."

"How is she?" he says, smiling broadly in recognition.

"Live and kicking," I say. I'm the one having a heart attack. I print his name under his signature. "My mother would pretend this was signed by a Martian if she couldn't decipher it."

"I understand," he says.

"I don't know a thing about the Living Bank except it has something to do with Dear Abby."

"Dear Abby has something to do with everything," Dr. Benedict says. "She's brought organ donation to the attention of her readers."

The two debating Unitarians are getting so heated that their supporters are forming into committees.

"Be sensitive to his argument," our hostess is saying.

We edge away from the group and park ourselves in front of a bowl of hummus and pita bread.

"What brings you to this festive event?" he says.

"I want to die organized," I say. "With my life and Living Will in order."

He looks intently at me, without speaking. He gives me the odd feeling of being outside myself. I feel we have everything in common, but on so subtle a level I can't figure out how to talk about it.

"Do you think Mrs. Fritz is going to die, Dr. Benedict?" I say, finally.

"She could be around for a long time yet," he says. "It's difficult to diagnose someone who faints like that. It's even worse when someone is what we call 'found down'—an unconscious body you don't know what to do with."

He's so earnest he almost looks as if he's frowning. He doesn't look unhappy, just serious. Web laughs all the time, but that doesn't mean he's happy. Dr. Benedict's high forehead looks chiseled out of stone. The bone bulges above his eyebrows, as if his skull needs the space for his enormous mind. He has a dimple in the middle of his frown, between his heavy blond eyebrows, right above his patrician nose.

"Dr. Benedict—" I say, addressing his dimple.

"Please, call me Gabriel," he says. His gaze captures mine, brings my eyes back to his.

I meditate on his name like a mantra. Gabriel, Gabriel. It's as if my heart has been speaking his name for years, but in some language I couldn't understand. "Gabriel," I say, worried I say it a little too softly, too lovingly. "Isn't working in the emergency room exhausting?"

"Not really," he says. "I work two weeks of twelve-hour shifts, then I take a day off." He looks tired, but in a rugged, manly way. He looks the way Achilles must have when he routed the Trojans, or Leif Ericson at the end of the day he discovered Vinland.

"How many patients come through in a day?" I say.

"Two to four hundred on the medical side, another couple of hundred on the surgical side," he says. "The worst thing is telling family members that the patient died. I have to do that a lot."

"How awful," I say.

"What do you do?" he says.

"My job is to get library books to the people who need them the most but don't know it," I say. "Would Service-to-the-Unserved help in the emergency waiting room?"

"It might," he says.

What would it be like to see him on a regular basis at the hospital? I stare at his wedding ring while the Unitarians debate behind me. The two sides of the debate sound like the good angel and the bad angel whispering in each of my ears. I struggle against my attraction for him—that mysterious, energizing spark.

"Are you a Unitarian?" I say, to try to get myself back on some sort of moral track.

"No," he says. "Although my views are eclectic."

"Is your wife Unitarian?"

"My wife," he says. He looks the way Lucifer must have when God said "You're fired."

He seems to forget I've asked the question, or even that

I'm there. He puts down his pita bread; I put down my cup. I peer at him, down a long tunnel of loneliness.

"My wife and I are divorcing," he says after a while.

"I'm sorry," I lie.

"That's all right," he says.

His wedding band looks like a horrible little halo. "You still wear your ring?" I say.

"I can't get it off," he says. "It's stuck."

"You could have it cut off," I say.

He looks at me as if I've suggested he get tattooed. "That's true," he says finally. "I don't need that finger anyway."

We rest in a blue spaciousness, quiet as the eye of a hurricane. I hear the meeting all around us, the Unitarians talking, a door opening, then closing, the soft step of a foot on the rug. I watch him put away huge quantities of pita bread again, as if it's all he'll get for dinner. His beeper goes off.

"Will you excuse me?" he says. He stands up to leave. He's so gorgeous, all six feet and four inches. Shoulders back, head high, he looks as if he never had a moment of poor posture in his life.

"Yes," I say, but I don't know what I'm saying. No, no, no, I want to say, stay here forever—with me.

His gaze lingers on my face. Again I'm stabbed by the feeling that he loves me, I love him. How can this be? I don't believe in love at first or second sight. I hardly believe in love at all.

He walks toward the door. He turns to give me a little wave.

Tears sting my eyes. Isn't it the beauty in nature that speaks to us of our goodness, the way a tree yellow with autumn lights up the heart? Is that Aristotle or Shirley MacLaine?

7

New Age Hostages

I sit at St. Francis's kitchen table with Gigi, Barbara, and Mrs. Fritz. Gabriel's in the back of my mind, Dolores in the front of it. "What kind of job do you suppose Dolores had if becoming a manicurist would be a step up?" I say.

"You're obsessing on Dolores," Gigi says. "We feel sorry for her, but we don't even know her."

"I wonder whether she has kids to worry about," I say.

"Why don't you ask her?" Barbara says, smoothing her skirt over her pregnant abdomen.

"It's really none of my business," I say.

"That's never stopped *me*," she says. "Loan officers ask people all kinds of things that are none of their business. That's how I got where I am today."

"Pregnant?" Gigi says.

"Promoted," Barbara says, frowning at her.

"Dolores is quick on the uptake," I interject. "She could be anything she wanted if she had an education, job training, an exercise program, a makeover."

"A makeover is not going to help someone with all those other problems," Gigi says.

"You're probably right," I groan. "But it's too late, I just submitted my proposal."

"For prisoner makeovers?" Gigi says incredulously.

"As part of a prisoner fashion show, to improve their self-images," I say. "I wrote that proposal under PMS."

"You must have been really hormonally spaced out," Barbara says. "If you were pregnant, you'd be dangerous."

In spite of her hearing problem, Mrs. Fritz picks up that I'm worried about one of my Service-to-the Unserved patrons. "Why don't you move her into the Lord's Motel?" she says.

"I can't, she's in jail," I say.

"Jail!?" Mrs. Fritz says.

"Remember them that are in bonds, as bound with them; and them which suffer adversity, as being yourselves also in the body," St. Francis says. "That's Hebrews 13:3."

Gigi rolls her eyes.

St. Francis clears our drained juice glasses. He bears witness to our various preoccupations. I suddenly see him as just a lonely guy.

"We don't want to hear any more about Dolores," Gigi says. "It's too depressing."

Gigi and I head upstairs together to our apartments, then stand in the hall between them. We're so rushed neither of us wants to commit to a sitting-down conversation anymore. The suspension would be like Limbo except that our suffering makes it more like Purgatory.

"You'll never guess who I saw at the Unitarian party," I say. "Gabriel."

Gigi looks blank, then her eyeliner widens around her dark eyes. She looks like a cross between a puppy and a femme fatale. "Dr. Benedict?" she says. "What was a nice man like him doing in a place like that?"

"It was a party about death and he's getting a divorce," I say.

"Oh," she says, taking a cigarette from the pack in her purse and lighting it. "That explains everything." She leans back against the railing, crosses her delicate ankles, looks expectantly at me.

"You have to quit smoking, Gigi," I say.

"I know," she says, holding her hand in front of the wispy smoke as if she can create her own Smoking section right here at the top of the stairs. "So what did he say? What did *you* say?"

I worry that St. Francis will come out of his downstairs apartment, smell Gigi's cigarette, and evict her on the spot. "We talked about Mrs. Fritz," I say. "We talked about his work in the emergency room."

"Of course," she says. "But what about his *divorce?* Did he ask you *out?*"

"If it'd been you, I know you two would be engaged by now," I say. "But don't be ridiculous, he's not interested in *me*. Besides, he's not divorced yet, he's still in the middle of it."

She burns a loose thread off her sleeve with the glowing tip of her cigarette. "Look, Colleen," she says. "Every man has a big problem. If you want a man at all you have to figure out what kind of big problem you're willing to deal with."

"I have to solve my big problem with Web first," I say.

Gigi coughs on her exhale, then waves the blue-gray cloud down the stairs. When we were best friends at Our Lady of Perpetual Sorrows, Gigi and I smoked on the roof of the convent attached to the school. We found a secret stairway with only one dangerous part—through the nuns' cloister. We slipped off our squeaky brown loafers; the gray linoleum steps felt cool. At the top of the cloister's back stairs was a trap door that opened onto the roof. We crawled out, tearing our nylons on the shingles. We could see the entire grounds.

The softball team in their bright blue gym shorts ran across the grassy schoolyard. Below us, on the convent side, the nuns' laundered habits flapped black and white on the clotheslines. The nuns strolled in silence up and down the garden walks, reading their breviaries. We were ecstatic with longing—but for what, we didn't know.

"Don't be so compulsive and organized," Gigi says. "Web isn't the library."

"I just want to reassure myself I can have a regular love-life with Web before I screw up a brand-new relationship," I say. "I want to find the connection between love and sex."

"Look at *me,*" she says. "I had zero sex life with my ex-*husband,* and now Jack and I do it three times a week. How often do you think you should get fucked?"

"Three times a week seems reasonable," I say.

"Once a week is the national average," she says. "There's this new yuppie disease of not fucking at all because of two-career burnout. Why don't you get a seventeen-year-old and be done with Web?" She flicks her ashes into a tiny portable ashtray she carries in her purse.

I never smoked much, but I stopped completely when I began to run marathons with Web. Aerobic wheezing seemed counterproductive. "I don't want a seventeen-year-old, I want an adult male. Anyway, fucking is beginning to seem disgusting to me. The body is disgusting—all muck and ooze."

"Muck and ooze? Did you make that up?"

"It sounds like James Joyce, doesn't it."

"Men never talk to each other like this," she says.

"I'm afraid to even fantasize about Gabriel," I say. "I don't want to cultivate that mind-state."

"There's nothing wrong with fantasizing," she says. "The world runs on fantasies."

"That's what's wrong with it. I have this horrible feeling

we're creating the world with what we think, but nobody wants to take responsibility for it."

"I can't live across the hall from someone who's New Age," Gigi says, crushing the end of her cigarette on the sole of her elegant pump. She puts the stub in the ashtray, then carefully puts the ashtray back in her purse.

"New Age is too weird even for me," I say. "It reminds me of digging a hole to China."

"Lower your voice," she says. "St. Francis might hear us."

We hug each other and go into our apartments.

It's one of those warm Houston evenings when the cicadas sound like ringing telephones. I take a mug of PMS tea out to the parking lot to sit in one of the lawn chairs. St. Francis got the chairs at a discount store for $4.99 each. He re-webs their plastic seats from time to time. I pick up a chair and shake off the hard berries that fall from the tree above. The black cat underneath gets indignant and stalks away, followed by a sympathetic calico cat from one chair over. These cats definitely have an attitude.

St. Francis comes out and slaps raw liver down on the back step. All the cats, except one small, scrawny red one, rush to it.

"Why won't she eat?" I ask St. Francis.

"She's in transition," he says. "Her old pleasures are disappointing but she's got nothing to replace them."

He feeds the pigeons flapping back and forth from the top of the carport to the power lines. He keeps their barrel of sunflower seeds in his bedroom closet. He goes back in.

I sip tea and struggle to sort out my feelings about Web and Gabriel. I belong to that small minority of people who still haven't got things figured out. Everyone in New York already knows everything. It's like the hierarchy of reading groups in grade school. There were the Cardinals, then the Bluebirds, then the few slow readers whose group wasn't named because no one wanted the stigma of belonging to it. We should have been named something small and brown. The Sparrows.

Barbara comes out, three months pregnant now. She plunks down in the lawn chair next to mine; I hear a piece of webbing snap beneath her. I like Barbara, but I can't talk to her the way I can to Gigi. Barbara's so wholesome in her blond, big-boned way. She has birthing hips; she has probably looked maternal her whole life. I wonder if her baby will have eyes like hers, the color of Texas bluebonnets.

"How do you feel?" I say.

"Overpopulated," she laughs. It comes out as sort of a hiccough, as if the baby goes into reverse, finds the way blocked, then scrambles forward again.

I can't imagine having a baby with Web. I feel pebbles in my uterus just thinking about it. I take a gulp of my tea.

"What are you drinking?" Barbara says.

"PMS tea," I say. "Dandelion root and herbal diuretics."

"Do you have premenstrual syndrome?" she says.

"Not at the moment, but maybe if I drink PMS tea all month long it won't hit so hard. St. Francis told me to get it at Whole Paycheck Health Foods. Want some?"

"It won't help in my condition," she says. "Nothing does."

The cats are thinking of reinstating themselves under our lawn chairs. They crowd in under Barbara and the baby sleeping somewhere in the soft pillows of her plumpness. I wonder whether Gabriel wants children, or whether he already has them.

"How are you feeling about the baby?" I say.

"I'm resolved about it, I guess," Barbara says. "St. Francis has us all on some sort of spiritual modular learning plan; I can't even squash a bug anymore. I caught a June bug in a cup and slid my hurricane warning instructions under it, then while I was kicking open the back door and congratulating myself for my compassion, I dropped it and scared the cats. Cats as meditative as these are very hyper when disturbed."

St. Francis would be gratified to know the Lord's Motel is having a good effect on at least one of us. "But you saved the June bug," I say. "That was good."

"I could never have an abortion," she says.

"No," I say.

"Everybody used to in the seventies," she says.

"Yes," I say.

"Even in the sixties, when it was illegal."

"Yes," I say, "except those who had acid babies."

"What were acid babies?" she says.

"Their mothers took tabs of purple haze or orange sunshine instead of the Pill. I saw one once. 'This is Raphael,' his mother said. 'He's an acid baby.' He was beatific-looking—this big pale head and enormous blue eyes."

"What became of the acid babies?" Barbara says.

"They're serving on city councils all over America," I say.

Barbara leans back in her lawn chair. "Would you have had an abortion if you were me?" she says.

"Probably not," I say. "Bad karma."

"Not to mention it might be my last chance," she says.

"Most of us are worrying whether we'll ever get married and have babies. You're doing it a little bit out of order but at least you're doing the baby part."

"But I'd just passed out of the regret at not having a child into thinking I got off easy," she says.

"I know what you mean," I say. "I'm beginning to realize that it's something life's not going to require of me."

"Famous last words," Barbara says.

"Do you wish you could marry the welder?" I ask.

"How can I?" she says. "I don't even know his address. There are some things you can't find out about a man after you sleep with him, so find out everything you want to know first."

A squirrel shaking the branch above me knocks berries into my lap. I fret about all the things I'll never understand about Web. Should I kiss having babies goodbye? Getting to know Gabriel seems impossible, never mind sleeping with him. "Sometimes I think I should find one of those nice comfortable men, a little pudgy, who's grateful and adoring," I say. "Instead of looking for one of those superstar glamour boys who just wants you to watch while he conquers the world and becomes the best whatever."

"If you found one of the nice pudgy ones, would you marry him?" she says.

"I don't know," I say, wondering whether Barbara's welder is pudgy. "My family wants me to get married to anyone so the wedding would bring a little excitement into their lives."

"Marriage must be like having a parent who tells you *what* you can't do, *when* you can't do it, *where* you can't do it, *how* you can't do it, and with *whom* you can't do it," she says.

"What about the Betty Crocker dream of living with a man you love—cooking breakfast, lunch, and dinner, and creating a calm, happy refuge for you both?" I say.

Barbara stands up so quickly she knocks over the lawn chair. The cats scatter in alarm. "Women's minds have got so much more complex than men's that the men are helpless in relationships. To retaliate, vast numbers of men have vacated the field and effectively wrested power from the women by reducing the numbers of men available. So loan officers like me are forced to get impregnated by welders using pay phones."

I'd be terrified to apply for a loan from Barbara. "When

you put it like that," I say, "I guess I can't see myself sitting quietly with Web in the evening."

"Of course not," she says. "You're just trying to tide yourself over with the wrong man until the right one comes along. And I'm still looking for the wrong man."

She heads back to her apartment as if she can't waste another second.

I go back up to my apartment and call Mrs. Fritz, downstairs. If I can't be connected with Gabriel, I can be connected with Mrs. Fritz who's connected with him. After all, he probably saved her life.

She always answers the phone feebly so telephone solicitors won't bug her. It scares me to hear her sound so much on her last legs. If I ever get an answering machine, I'll have her rasp the recorded message: "We can't...come to the phone...but we'll be happy...to call you back...if we ain't *dead*...by then."

"Come on down," she hoots now. "I'm just wearing a hole in the sofa."

"Would tomorrow be better?" I say.

"Come down now!" she says. "Today's a sure thing."

When I get there, she's standing in the doorway taking delivery on her bucket of Kentucky Fried Chicken while St. Francis looks on disapprovingly. "St. Francis," she says, "I don't have a man, so I'm entitled to my Kentucky Fried Chicken."

"Why don't you get a man?" he says.

"I don't want a man," she says. "I'd rather have meat!"

"God will let you know when you're ready to give up meat," he says, trudging back into his apartment.

"I'm a vegetarian, but I'd rather have a man," I say.

Mrs. Fritz's white hair floats in a cirrus cloud across her head. Her ice-blue eyes stare at me but I don't know whether she can see me or not. Each day she looks more like her gerbil, squinting. She wears her glasses like a necklace. It wouldn't surprise me if she could see through her Third Eye. She puts her bony fingers on my arm and reads me like braille.

"I've brought some cantaloupe and blueberries," I holler so she can hear me, putting them down to give her a hug. She's so fragile I feel like Batman, towering over her and spreading my arms like a cape.

"Let's eat them right away," she says. "St. Francis is taking me to the grocery store tomorrow but I had no idea what I was going to eat in the meantime except for my Kentucky Fried Chicken."

Maybe when you're ninety-five you don't have extra food around in case you don't live to eat it. I try to figure out how to bring up all the questions I have about her medical condition. "I saw Dr. Benedict at a Unitarian party about death and dying," I say, as we sit down at her dining room table.

"How's your relationship with him going?" she says.

"What relationship?" I say. "He's in the middle of a divorce." I've arranged the blueberries in the hollow of the melon; some of these spill out and roll across the table.

She stares into her cantaloupe to see where to dig in with her spoon. "Don't worry, dearie, men who are getting divorced are up and down the first year," she says. "Then the second year they look around. If your relationship is deep enough, he'll come back to you after that. It takes two years."

"How do you know so much about it?" I say.

"I married several of them before I turned to Kentucky Fried Chicken," she says, giving up on the melon and starting in on a chicken thigh. "Now, let's get back to you and Dr. Benedict."

She wants to talk about Gabriel and me; I want to talk about Gabriel and her. I'm ignorant not only of her medical condition, but of her final wishes. There are some things you can't find out about someone after she dies. "The Unitarian party was about medical directives to physicians," I say, bumbling into the subject. "It was about artificial life support and organ donation."

"You shouldn't be fretting about things like that, dearie," she says. "You should be thinking about getting married and having babies."

"That's *all* I think about," I say. "But what about *you?*"

"Why should I think about getting married and having babies?" she says. "Let's have a drink."

We begin our journey toward the kitchen. Her balance is unimaginably terrible; every few steps I think she's going over. I hope she never drinks and walks.

"How have you been since you fainted?" I say, taking another tack.

"I have the vapors, that's all," she says.

"What *are* the vapors?" I say.

"It means you feel like shit," she says. "I'd better have iced tea, or Dr. Benedict will be pissed." She pulls out the ice cube tray and throws it in the sink. She reaches into the cupboard for two tall tumblers, then fingers a jar of knives on the counter. The knives are blade side up. She draws one out and saws off two sprigs of mint from the plant on her windowsill.

I carry our frosty glasses of iced tea into the dining room and set them down on the lace tablecloth. "What if you faint again?" I say, with more urgency.

"Dearie, there's nothing wrong with me but a few aches and pains," she says, "and they're from getting in and out of bed."

"I have the same problem," I say, nearly defeated.

"There's a right way to get in and out of bed," she says. "It says so on the milk carton."

She wobbles to her refrigerator, takes out a half-gallon of milk, brings it back to the table. On the side of the carton are illustrated instructions on how to hoist yourself up on your elbow and swing your legs over the bed without straining your back.

"That's not exactly what I meant," I say.

"Now, if the milk people would tell us how to get rid of the vapors," she says.

"How did you get the vapors?" I say.

"Housecleaning," she says.

"We should get someone to do it for you," I say.

"I like to do it myself," she says.

I look around and wonder how dirty it could get. "How long does it take you?" I say.

"It'd take a whole day, including rest stops," she says. "But usually I do a little every day, then start over."

"I do mine room by room," I say. "The kitchen, the bathroom, the bedroom, the living room."

"I dust all at once, then I vacuum all at once," she says.

"The trouble is," I say, "it doesn't stay clean for long."

"Bleach and ammonia," she says. "Not together, of course—they make a gas that'll kill you."

At last the conversation has come back around to death. I gulp my iced tea. The ice cubes are gone now. "Mrs. Fritz—" I begin.

"Tea stains our stomachs, you know," she interrupts.

With her indomitable will, Mrs. Fritz has defeated my best efforts to discuss her fragile health. Perhaps she's afraid talking about it will send her careening into death. She walks me to the door. On the way she goes on tilt. She grabs onto the doorjamb and holds on tightly, then drops her head and gasps for air.

"I'm all right," she says.

•

That night, the air hangs heavy in the trees outside my window. I dream that I marry Gabriel, on a gardenia-scented evening pierced by fireflies. My wedding gown is white lace with a long train and blush veil. Looking plucked from the top of our wedding cake, Gabriel is devastatingly handsome in his tux. Gigi is my maid of honor, Barbara and Mrs. Fritz my bridesmaids, all in Blessed Mother blue. We marry at the Unitarian church that sponsored the Living Bank party where we met. St. Francis walks me down the aisle, giving me away from the Lord's Motel. Our reception is at the Lord's Motel, the doors open to all our candlelit apartments. Strolling musicians play romantic music; the guests dance under the stars in the parking lot. Everyone's there—Dolores, Lieutenant Sprunt, Joanne, and Ralph. My mother and father are in the same place together for the first time in twenty years, and my family is pleasantly surprised I've married so well. But the best part is the kiss Gabriel gives me at the altar, so passionate that the congregation gasps.

8

Linguine Lingerie

Web's ship calls in Galveston one Saturday, and he talks me into meeting him there. He'd have a girl in every port if I didn't go to every port to be the girl. I drive south on I-45, descend into Galveston's faded decadence. I drive past the bait shops, the seafood markets, the oleander bushes with their poisonous pink blossoms. Steamy air hangs like ghosts over peeling clapboard Victorian houses, the former inhabitants guilty of terrible sins. The hurricane shutters on some of the houses are nailed shut.

Web has booked us a suite at the Mermaid, an old luxury resort hotel on the furthest reach of the island.

"I heard they were renovating this," I say to him.

"They were just laundering money," he says.

After we check in I undress and rummage around in the bag of expensive resort clothes Web brought for me. I thought maybe if I let him orchestrate my luggage he'd take better care of it.

"Where is the nightgown?" I say.

"We can take a nap on the beach," he says, and pulls out a lace bikini for me.

"It's all holes," I say.

"It's linguine lingerie," he says. "After you wear it we can eat it."

We go out and lie down on the warm white sand. In front of a red and white cabana there's a sign like a lemonade stand's that says "Punk Psychoanalysis."

"You'd expect that in California but not in Galveston," I say.

The seagulls swoop and dive; my ear hears only its own high cries. The Gulf is striated blue and green, different depths. I've been seeing Web this way for three years now. How much would that add up to in real time, if we had a normal relationship like everyone else? What would I understand about him?

"What did you do between Princeton and becoming a cruise-ship social director?" I say.

"I worked for my father," he says.

"Doing what?" I say.

"He made me a vice president of his company," he says.

"What kind of company was it?" I say.

"Imports and exports," he says.

Five seagulls sit on five pilings where the Gulf hits the shore. They puff out their white breasts, hold their gray wings stiffly at their sides. A sixth seagull circles and dive-bombs, knocks off one of the other seagulls, and takes his place. The displaced seagull knocks off another seagull. They do this over and over.

"Why doesn't the extra seagull find a piling somewhere else?" I say.

"It's a dominance game," Web says.

The sun pours down. It's hard to believe the bad rays can't get through our sunscreen.

"What did you do as a vice president?" I ask Web after a while.

"Came in late and left early," he says.

"Sounds fun," I say. "So you left to go to sea?"

"It was either that or law school," he says, shuddering.

Somewhere in Web is the reason he won't make love the normal way. He makes me feel my longing for love is annoyingly legalistic. "Why don't you want to make regular love to me?" I say.

"Colleen, I like you," he says. "Why do you have to keep bringing it up? God, the pressure!"

"But you don't love me, you don't want to make *love*," I say. "You don't really care about me."

"It's nothing to talk about," he says. "Let's just lie here on the beach. Talk about it some other time, if you have to. You take all the romance out of it."

I hate feeling as if I have to beg for it. I lie there on the hot sand. "Maybe I should just go back to Houston," I say, sitting up to gather my things.

Web props himself up on one arm. He doesn't really want to be with me, but he doesn't want me to leave, either. "I'm sorry," he says, sounding depressed. "I'm not too good at the one-on-one. I don't know why."

"Have you really never been married?" I say.

"Never," he says.

We stare out at the Gulf. I wonder what kind of marriage his parents had, and what his life with his parents was like. Did he not like imports and exports, or not like working for his father?

"Maybe I could meet your father sometime," I say.

"I don't see him much," he says. "Not since my mother died."

"I'm sorry your mother died," I say. "How old were you?"

"I was already working for my father," he says.

The seagulls leave the pilings in a group; they flap out over the waves.

Web watches them with an unhappy look in his eyes. "My mother died in the Gulf of Mexico."

The gulls disappear into the muggy air. The day grows into the most quiet one in history. We hear not even our own breath. The air hangs, as if the breeze descended halfway and forgot.

"My parents were on a cruise," he goes on in a miserable tone. "My father's mistress was in the next stateroom."

The sun turns black.

"Did your mother know?"

"She drowned," Web whispers.

I see his mother hurtling overboard, down the side of the ship into the black water. The dance band was playing, couples whirled under the stars.

He lies back down on the sand.

"I'm so sorry," I say.

"Ssshhh," he says.

It's what he says when I want to talk in bed. The waves start far out and roll in one at a time. They make a hollow sound, not like water. On the sand bars, sssshhhh ... sssshhhh ... sssshhhh.

He falls asleep. I cover him with a beach towel so he won't get burned. The sun is warm and horrible. I'm so tired. I lie beside him and fall in and out of sleep. What good children we are, Web and I. We're stick figures. My mouth is full of sand. Wind me up and I'm nice. I'm/so/glad/to/meet/yew, smile, smile. Web in his navy blue blazer, white shirt, gray trousers. Yes/sir. No/ma'am. His shoes are shined; he holds the door open for ladies; his handshake is firm. I want his mother to come back and see he does everything she told him.

When he stirs, I wake with a start. "I tucked you in," I say.

"Did you kiss me goodnight?" he says.

"No," I say.

"My mother loved me," he says.

"I know," I say.

"She put notes in my lunch box," he says.

"Yes," I say.

We get up and walk back into our hotel, like robots. The late afternoon and evening is like that. We eat our expensive dinner mechanically. The dining room is cavernous, with high ceilings and dark walls.

"Everything is so—*much*," Web says, rubbing his hand across the velvet seat, picking up the heavy silver fork.

"It's a sin to pay twenty-five dollars for a salad and sixty dollars for a piece of fish," I say.

I'm possessed by our fear. By keeping it at a distance from myself, I see I'm not afraid of Web, nor he of me. We're accomplices. We do as we're told. But we collude with each other to keep it from killing us.

"You've never been to this kind of party before," Web says later when he leads me into a windowless private party room as if I'm some sort of glamorous celebrity. Crowds of drinking, smoking men part to let us through.

"There are no other women here," I say to Web.

"It's a stag party," he says.

At least there aren't any other women for him to ogle. He ushers me into a wine cellar, where he pulls things out of the bag he brought. Weird black lace lingerie, with holes where the nipples and crotch would be.

"What's so great about black anyway?" I ask.

"White women are supposed to wear black lace, and black women look best in red lace," he says.

"How do you know these things?" I ask him.

He puts a mask over my face, a black one with plumes, and thrusts a feathery black fan at me.

"Dance," he says.

He pushes me gently out the wine cellar door into the party room. I think of resisting but I want Web to love me.

Disco music starts somewhere, a hush falls over the rowdy men. My heart pounds; I try to pretend it's pleasure. I wiggle and slide to the pulsating beat. It's horrifying how I know how to do what comes unnaturally. Web is somewhere watching me.

The music plays, the singer sings. I'm trying to split open, like a husk. I give in to the music, and I dance. Sometimes I dream that Web loves me. I dance our love and our loss, give in to the beautiful death, into the ecstasy of nothing left to lose. The music heads toward its crest. I twirl and spin in my black lace. I hold the black feather fan above my head, high over my plumed mask. Whirling faster and faster on my black spike heels, I catch bits of the world as it rushes by. The men are a blur around me.

Cascades of music break over me. The men get out of hand. Their faces darkening as ominously as thunderclouds, they come toward me with a slow rumble. Their eyes burn with lust. I freeze, terrified.

Web rushes up and escorts me away, up a back elevator. He hands me my clothes and puts a Thermos bottle of champagne into my shaking hands. He's famous to me for loving Thermos bottles and I'm famous to him for loving champagne.

"How do you get involved with these people?" I say.

"I'm the *social* director," he says. "I orchestrate interesting activities for the ship's passengers. The groom and his ushers are waiting for you."

"Oh, no," I say. "Why should I do this?"

"Why do you do anything?" he says.

"To have the experience?" I say.

"All right, then," he says.

We step out of the elevator into the penthouse Honeymoon Suite. Four men stand around in the sitting room. They look sheepish, like fraternity hogs. Web hands me four condoms.

"Safe sex?" I say. "This whole thing imperils my immortal soul." I resolve not to go through with this, even though my New Year's resolution was to be less resolved. Would God frown on my praying my way out of it?

"The groom first," Web says.

The guys push him forward and, before I know it, we're in the bedroom. "There's been a mistake," I begin when he shuts the door.

"No problem," he says. "I'm getting hitched tomorrow and I got to save my strength, if you know what I mean."

"The truth is," I say, "I'm a librarian."

"For real?" he says. "My fiancée's a librarian."

We chat nervously about where she went to library school and how she wants to arrange his comic-book collection by Dewey decimals.

"How'd she do in Cataloging and Classification?" I say.

"I'm sketchy on that," he says.

"You should find that out before you marry her," I say.

We sit there silently, listening to the men in the other room get rowdy. I worry they'll attract the wrath of the hotel management. The guys applaud when he goes out.

I look around the Honeymoon Suite, at the pink and red everything. Even the Jacuzzi is pink marble veined with gold. I'm as far from the Lord's Motel as I can be. Have I come this far from the mind of God so I can begin, at last, the long journey back? I doubt it. I'm perched anxiously on the edge of the water bed when the best man comes in and sits in a heart-shaped chair.

"I can't go through with this," I say.

"That's okay, I don't do it with girls anyway," he says.

"Aren't you worried about AIDS?" I say.

"I don't do it with guys either," he says. "I'm asexual."

"What an interesting equivocation," I say. "I'm thinking of taking up asexuality myself."

"We're listed in the *Directory of American Associations*," he says. "You can write for our literature."

"Why did you get in line for my nookie?" I say.

"The other guys don't know—most asexuals aren't out of the closet," he says. "But we do have an asexual running for Congress."

"Then there's reason for optimism," I say.

"Don't forget to register to vote," he says on his way out.

So far I've got off easy, but I'm still green with fright when the third, an usher, comes in.

"What's the matter?" he says.

"Just a little seasick," I say.

"They didn't tell me it was a water bed," he says.

"They had other things on their minds," I say.

"I don't want to do it, I just want to pretend I'm doing it while I suffocate you," he says, pushing me down on the water bed, squashing a pillow over my face. I can't breathe. I'm going to die, and in mortal sin. I push him off me, as if bench-pressing two hundred pounds.

"Easy," he says, backing off. "I didn't want to suffocate you, I just wanted to *pretend* to suffocate you."

"Your time's up," I gasp, trying not to have a nervous breakdown. "Out."

Now the perverts are perverting their perversions. If I wait long enough, maybe they'll come full circle and be what used to pass for normal. I'm shaking on the edge of the water bed when the fourth guy comes in. He's so huge I think of Catherine the Great when the crane broke and the horse fell on her. He dives onto the water bed. It bursts. I scream.

"What's the matter?" Web says, tearing in.

"My water broke," I say.

The usher crawls out of the broken bed on all fours, lumbers out of the room like a big, wet bear.

"You made a fortune," Web says, pulling me out and handing me a wad of cash. "Enough to put yourself through college except that you've already put yourself through college many times."

"I don't want the money," I sputter.

"You have to take it," he says. "It's part of it."

The floodwaters begin to recede through the floor. Soaking wet from head to toe, I look as if I've come straight from the pool. I peel off my wet lace and look around desperately for a complimentary terry cloth robe.

"Would you hold my money?" I say, handing it back to Web. "I'd tuck it away somewhere except I've no place to tuck it."

The members of the wedding party are shoving each other out the door when a vice officer arrives, out of breath. He takes in my dishabille. He's one panting man too many tonight.

Web hands the now-wet wad of cash back to me, grins apologetically. He turns away as smoothly as if he's doing a cha-cha step.

"Where are you going?" I cry.

"My ship sails in a few minutes," he says in his conspiratorial whisper.

"You can't just leave me here like this," I say.

"Please don't make a scene," he whispers, his shoulders rising to his ears. He tiptoes down the hall after the fraternity hogs.

Dressed in water, I'm still gazing at the space where he was when the hotel manager appears.

"The water leaked down to the suite below," he says to the vice officer. "Is this what it looks like?"

"Ma'am," the officer says, handcuffing my hands behind me after I dress, "you have the right to remain silent." He recites my rights as if they're the Twenty-third Psalm. "The Lord is my shepherd; I shall not want. Anything you say can and will be used against you in a court of law.... He leadeth me in the paths of righteousness. You have a right to talk to a lawyer and have him present with you while you are being questioned.... Yea, though I walk through the valley of the shadow of death.... If you cannot afford to hire a lawyer.... Surely goodness and mercy shall follow me all the days of my life.... one will be appointed to represent you.... And I will dwell in the house of the Lord forever."

The manager rushes past me into the bedroom to survey the burst water bed while the vice officer mumbles into his radio for a "wagon call," my transport to jail. He and the manager escort me down in the freight elevator. The manager rocks on his heels. We go out the delivery entrance. A patrol car screeches to a halt and two police officers get out.

"This way, please, ma'am," one of them says. His exaggerated politeness frightens me. Either he thinks I'm a feminist spy for the ACLU, or he's masking the violence of what's about to happen.

I can't believe this is happening to me. I climb into the back of the police car while the other officer fills in the blanks on his clipboard form. My eye-level view is of the guns in the officers' holsters, wide black patent belts holding their middles together.

I start crying somewhere on the ride along the seawall. White crests crash over the black waves. The waves start so far out it takes them forever to break. They hesitate over the sand bars, then roll in, collapse, into their hollow sound. Through the police car window grate, Galveston looks like a trompe l'oeil, a front for a city, not the city itself. My love for Web is lost somewhere inside a city that doesn't exist.

9

Prisoner of the Month

The police car stops in a gated area behind the jail. I climb out at Prisoner Unloading.

"Female!" the police officer shouts, banging on the metal door.

He hands me over to a woman guard, like a nursery school driver handing me over to an indifferent babysitter. She takes the paperwork from the police officer, scans it, slaps a pink plastic band around my wrist. There are three stacks of wristbands—pink for girls, blue for boys, and red for AIDS.

I stand in the Female Holding Area with fifteen other women, some swearing, some weeping, others sullen.

"Y'all do not know how to treat a *lady,*" shrieks a tall transvestite in a miniskirt and bright red lipstick, while a guard searches him.

"Got a he-she down here for transfer to Men's," the guard says into the phone.

Everyone's afraid, the prisoners, the jittery guards. Addicts not in control of their nervous systems teeter on their pins.

"Hands on the counter," a female guard says to me, taking

off my handcuffs, then searching me with brisk authority. She puts my ring, my watch, my Kleenex into a canvas envelope, names each item as a clerk checks off a property list. She counts the wad of cash I sold my soul for.

"One thousand bucks," she whistles. She slides my property envelope under the glass counter window, while I give my name and Social Security number to the uniformed clerk behind the glass. The clerk types on a computer keyboard, presses a key to wait for a print-out of everything I've ever done wrong in the state of Texas.

The guard points to two worn white footprints painted on the concrete floor. They're flat, like the insoles of my aerobics shoes. The feet look vulnerable, their toes pointing out slightly. I miss my shoes. I put my feet in the footprints, stand in front of the inch markings on the wall for my photograph. I feel like crying, but would be ashamed to be crying in my photo. I wish I had my Kleenex back. I wish I were back at the Lord's Motel, I wish I were home with my shoes.

I sit on a hard bench in a holding cell while they process my paperwork. I'm afraid of the other women in the cell; some look as if they're about to explode. I wish Dolores were with me, she'd tell me what to do to survive here. The men's and women's cells are out of each other's line of sight; the men shout drunkenly over the women's din.

Jail guards come and go, pulling women out, locking new ones in. When my name is called, a guard locks me in the caged rear section of an elevator. We descend to a lower level. The elevator is an oasis of quiet.

"I'm goin' into freight when I come up for retirement," the guard sighs to the elevator operator. "Freight don't kick and freight don't talk back to you." She peels back the flap over her shirt pocket with a Velcro hiss, pulls out a cigarette. In spite of No Smoking signs everywhere, everyone but the prisoners is smoking.

"What happens now?" I ask when she leads me off the elevator.

"You get processed, is what," she says, blowing smoke through her nose.

"What was that I just was?" I say.

"That was only intake, honey," she says, inhaling.

I stand in another set of feet for my mug shot, this time both front and side, behind black numbers on a white board. One of those WANTED photos you see in the post office is on the wall.

"Her rap sheet up yet?" the police photographer says.

The guard hands her my arrest record, such as it is, and frowns at me. This is where my life is ruined, like my mother always said it would be.

"Wash your hands," the fingerprinting person says.

I wash them at a sink black with eternal grime. I dry my hands with a brown paper towel made of paper so recycled it's on its way back to being a tree. The girl ahead of me, a seventeen-year-old on crack, gives the fingerprinting technician such a hard time that he makes her go back and wash her hands again. She kicks the bottom door of the sink cabinet hard, it falls off, and dozens of empty aluminum soft drink cans clatter out.

Help me, Dolores, I pray, invoking her as patron saint of this violent place. When it's my turn, I stand at the inked fingerprinting wheel while the technician rolls my personalized print sheet into place. He tugs at each of my fingers, rolls it on the black wheel, prints each finger twice. He rolls down another sheet for my other hand. He's even rougher than my manicurist.

When I've been thoroughly identified as the criminal I am, the guard takes me to Housing on an upper floor. She leads me down a long corridor, past a cell crammed with women watching an overhead TV.

"Change the fucking channel!" a disheveled woman screams at the guard as we walk by.

"I'll have it on a better one next time you come," the guard yells back.

We pass the isolation cell; a woman thrashes on a plastic mat in the claustrophobic space. There's no TV in the cell to which I'm taken, just three women lying around in despair. The blond one comes to the front of the cell, an imploring look on her tear-stained face.

The guard lets me in, locks the heavy door, crisscrossed with metal bars. "You got an underwire in your bra?" she says. She stands outside the cell while I take off my bra without unbuttoning my blouse. I unhook it, reach up one sleeve to pull the shoulder strap down over my crooked elbow, like Houdini. I reach up my other sleeve and pull the bra out. The guard takes it, deftly removes the underwire, hands back my bra to me. She walks away.

There's nothing in the windowless cell but the beds riveted to the cinderblock wall, a tiny stainless steel sink, a toilet. This is a pocket of the world where God doesn't come.

The three other women in the cell surround me. I've never been so frightened in my life.

"What they catch you doing, cutie?" one says. She's heavy, the inseams of her shorts riding up her dimpled thighs.

"I'm charged with prostitution," I say. I have to tell her *something*, but I'm too rattled to make anything up.

She spits.

"That so?" says the second woman. She has a broad, flat

face, butch haircut. "I'm Hot Checks, she's Drugs, she's Aggravated Assault," she goes on, pointing first to the heavy woman, then to the other. They sound like the three Furies, introduced this way.

"I didn't actually do it," I say.

"That don't mean nothin'," she says.

The third woman studies me. She reminds me of a blond version of Dolores, except for a scar across her face from her temple to her chin.

"Where'd you learn to do that, with your bra?" she says.

"Stuck in traffic on the Houston freeway in August," I say, grateful for the change of subject.

"Can you put it back on that way?" she says.

I stand there, teach them how to slide out their bras. The woman who reminds me of Dolores learns first, helps the others. I get mine back on without removing my blouse, but it doesn't feel the same without the underwire.

"How long do they keep us in here?" I say. The worst thing about all this is not knowing what will happen next.

The woman who spat now snorts. "Two weeks, easy," she says.

I gasp.

"Shut the fuck up, Lou," the broad-faced woman says.

Other than letting me know it won't be two weeks, this isn't very illuminating. My social skills fail me. I back away, sit down on a bare mattress. I keep to myself, while Lou and the other woman argue, and the blond woman falls asleep. Seized with rage and disappointment, I can't believe Web just left me here. He's the only one who knows I'm in jail, and he's sailing away, into the Gulf of Mexico.

The stag party music plays over and over in my mind, taunting me. I thought if I were in jail like Dolores, I'd meditate and do yoga. Instead, it's all I can do to hold myself together. The bedlam. The threat of the people around me. The craziness of my own mind, my fear of the guards. Dolores's despair makes perfect sense now. How ridiculous my cheery efficiency must seem to her. The help I offer her seems so superficial. How can I help her when I can't help myself?

Hours later, the jail guard comes back. We all crowd toward the front of the cell. The other women resent that the guard has come for me, not them. Only the one who reminds me of Dolores manages sullenly to wave goodbye.

The guard takes me to the Exit Room, where I perch anxiously on the edge of a molded plastic chair until a woman in a glass booth motions to me. She's the Employee of the Month, according to a plaque on the wall behind her.

"Your bond is set," she says. "Five hundred dollars."

"Do you take Visa?" I say.

"You have the cash in your property envelope," she says.

I hate that money. I give her the five hundred dollars; she gives me back my things. I sign a receipt for them. I stand in more footprints for my exit photo. The feet seem familiar now.

I take a taxi to my car in the Mermaid parking lot. The taxi driver and I hardly speak, each numb with the night.

The muggy sea air leaves a tacky film on my skin. My car rusts before my eyes. I drive out of Galveston at four in the morning, past the closed gas stations, the neon-lit convenience stores, the sidewalks sticky with spilled beer and soda, gum. I pass the graveyards, clammy air curling and rising around the tombstones.

I race north on I-45 toward Houston, past the oil refinery towns of La Marque, Texas City. The refineries glow across the fields, orange flames belch into the night sky. Here, the smell of oil, the exhumed earth. My tires hiss on the freeway.

I scream, pound with flat palms on the steering wheel. Automatic coffee makers click on in the suburbs, Pasadena, South Houston. Houston rises out of the prairie like Emerald City. The Transco Tower beacon roams like a searchlight. Mustn't scream, mustn't cry. I drive into Houston's gray maze of overpasses, underpasses, going home.

10

The Third Eye

In the first blue light of morning, like dusk turned inside out, I sneak into the parking lot of the Lord's Motel. I've fallen out of the mind of God. At least I won't have to face St. Francis; he always meditates at dawn.

The building feels ominously quiet. Upstairs, I take my newspaper from the hall into my apartment. The morning paper documents the city's night of bad dreams. It all runs together—an abused child murders the unlicensed day care operator who embezzled his trust fund, then dumps him into an oil spill.

I think about my mother. She has called lately, waited for me to say something. She wants me to come home for a visit. At least I think she does, but I'm not sure. That's how it is with me and my mother; I never can get what she's feeling, so I spend a lot of time trying to figure out what she feels and what to do about it.

I take off my sleazy clothes and put on my oldest ones, faded blue sweatshirt and sweatpants. These are nothing clothes. I wear them to be invisible, to be quiet. Afraid to be alone, I go down and knock on Mrs. Fritz's door.

She doesn't answer. St. Francis hears me knocking, comes out into the hall. "The ambulance took Mrs. Fritz to the hospital again last night," he says. "Where were *you?*"

"What happened?" I cry.

"Fainted, like before," he says. "She was in the hall, waiting for the Kentucky Fried Chicken man. That's what fried chicken will do to you."

"Where are Gigi and Barbara?" I say, wanting to shake him.

"Still asleep, I guess," he says. "They sat up in the emergency room until after midnight waiting for Mrs. Fritz, but that Dr. Benedict said she had to stay in the hospital this time."

I drive straight to the hospital in my old clothes. I can't find a parking space in the tall spiral of the hospital garage. At the top, I start back down, follow a line of cars with the same problem. Some people panic and try to go the wrong way, forcing the rest of us to go up instead of down the exit ramp. The entire line of cars comes to a dead halt. Choking on exhaust fumes, I hover in first gear, one foot on the accelerator, moving the other between the brake and the clutch. I back down the ramp I came up as the cars behind me do, horns honking. I squeeze into a tiny parking space I wasn't at the right angle for before. If only I'd been home when Mrs. Fritz fainted, instead of with Web.

Mrs. Fritz dozes on her back, lost in her hospital bed. The loose yellow skin of her face drapes over her cheekbones. Her nose arcs like half a rainbow. One long hair juts out from her chin. Her mouth hangs open, her thin lips peel from the inside.

"Mrs. Fritz?" I say.

Her bony chest rises and falls. Her brow puckers across her Third Eye, as if she's trying to see her way into wherever it is she's going. It's dark inside her mouth, her nostrils.

"Mrs. Fritz," I say, panicking.

Her blind blue eyes flutter open. "Colleen," she moans, curving her hand around mine like a soft claw. "My insides are doing things I just don't understand."

I wrap my other hand around hers. She drifts off again. I stand there helplessly, wondering how she can sleep through the racket of the building renovation down the hall and the blaring TV on the other side of the cloth partition that separates her from her roommate. This hospital is an awful place to be sick. The white walls are mind-numbing, the institutional furniture cold. A brown plastic emesis basin, plastic pitcher, and cup of warm water sit on the cabinet next to her bed. She doesn't even have a window.

A chunky, harried nurse rushes in, her rubber-soled shoes sucking at the waxed linoleum. She apologizes for the construction noise and checks Mrs. Fritz's I.V. "I can tell which nurse put this I.V. in," she says. "She only knows how to find one vein." She takes Mrs. Fritz's pulse, wakes her up to take her temperature.

"They're sorry about the noise," I shout to Mrs. Fritz when the nurse leaves.

"I don't hear it," she says. She drops my hand, gropes in the sheets as frantically as her weakness allows. "Where's my buzzer?"

I put the call buzzer into her hand.

"I throw up if I'm not holding onto it," she sighs.

She drifts off again. I match my breathing with hers, try to find the secret of her fainting. I fainted in church throughout my adolescence. I sat through High Mass, weak from fasting for Holy Communion, sustaining the tedium of the sermon. Breathing the expelled breath of sweating men and ladies in hats and girdles, I stared at the altar while its peripheries grew seasick green. The priest raised the Host, the dark green circle of light shrank. It blackened; I fainted.

"Ooohh," Mrs. Fritz moans when she wakes again, a desperate, animal sound. "What time is it?"

"Eight o'clock, Sunday morning," I say. "But the date on your calendar is wrong, that's tomorrow's date."

"I told them to tear off Sunday early," she says. "I got tired of looking at it."

Sundays are what we've done to spirit, turned it into a stale concept. The ions are all screwed up; the day is the soul of absence. Sundays my father visited us in our housing project, after my mother left him. Too frightened to enjoy the doughnuts he brought, we tried to force them down while we pretended to read the comics.

"But what happens tomorrow when you're tired of *it?*" I say.

"The hell with it," she says, and dozes off again.

Gabriel comes in. "Colleen!" he says, warmly shaking my hand. He looks pale and tired; no doubt he was up all night. His navy blue tie is rumpled—the black whales imprinted on it seem to swim in a restless sea.

"She says she throws up if she doesn't hold onto that buzzer thing," I say, hoping he won't ask where I was when Mrs. Fritz was brought in. I get up to give him my seat.

"She gets anxious if she feels isolated, abandoned," he says.

"I'm not going to abandon her," I say.

"I'm not either," he says, piercing me softly with his gaze.

"What happened last night?" I say. "How is she?"

"Her heart rhythm went out of whack," he says. "We pushed electricity through it with a cardiac defibrillator to stop the quivering."

"Quivering?" I say.

He tears his eyes away, looks at Mrs. Fritz. "We'll do more tests this week to find out why."

Mrs. Fritz stirs.

"How are you feeling, Mrs. Fritz?" he says, taking her hand.

"Am I glad to see *you*," she rasps. "You're handier than a shirt pocket."

My eyes flip to his shirt pocket; his prescription pad fits it perfectly.

"Have the nurses been turning you on a regular basis?" he asks Mrs. Fritz.

"I can't remember," she says wearily.

Maybe he could mark her, the way parking meter police do tires. Gabriel examines her while I listen to her roommate's TV. Her roommate is an unseen, unknowable presence, flipping the channels from one televised Sunday church service to another. The Baptists, the Catholics, the Presbyterians. Organ music and televangelists, then back to the Baptists again.

I feel suddenly exhausted. Last night in Galveston seems like a nightmare. "I'll be back tomorrow after work," I promise Mrs. Fritz. I lean over and hug her. I'm embarrassed to have Gabriel see me in my oldest clothes.

Gigi and Barbara give me the blow-by-blow of Mrs. Fritz's fainting, her trip to the hospital, their hours in the emergency waiting room.

"We were petrified," Barbara says. "Where were you?"

"In Galveston, with Web," I say.

"How is she?" Gigi says.

"Not good," I say.

They promise to visit Mrs. Fritz on their lunch hours tomorrow. St. Francis is upset but can't bring himself to go to the hospital. He thinks people are sick because they think they are, or because they've done something awful to themselves like eat meat. He gives me some medicinal white willow bark to take to Mrs. Fritz.

Gigi and I have a furtive discussion at the top of the stairs.

She chain-smokes nervously while I fill her in about the stag party with Web, how narrowly I wiggled out of selling my body, how I got arrested anyway and spent the night in jail.

"You could lose your job if you get convicted," she hisses.

"I know," I cry, about to collapse from fear and exhaustion.

"Try not to panic," she says. "You could get a job selling computer software."

"I don't know a thing about it," I say.

"You don't have to," she says. "You just have to know how to sell."

I go into my apartment to answer the phone. "Hello?" I say.

"Hello?" my mother says, as if I had called *her*.

She doesn't come out and ask me to come home for a visit. I don't invite myself because it doesn't seem like my home anymore. Shouldn't she do the inviting? I wish I knew whether this was hard because she doesn't express her feelings or because I'm too obtuse to get it.

I go to the hospital on Monday straight from work. Mrs. Fritz has little pads stuck to her chest, wires running from them to a tape recorder she wears on a strap. It looks like a high-tech disco bag.

"What's that for?" I ask her, alarmed.

"Ask Dr. Benedict when he gets here," she sighs. "He's my boss."

It's dinnertime, but she hasn't touched the tray next to her bed. "How do you like the hospital food?" I say.

"It's fine if you like breakfast at ten, lunch at two, and dinner at four," she says.

"Don't you want some of this nice orange Jello?" I say.

"I'm not supposed to eat or drink anything anyway," she says as Gabriel lopes in, grinning as if he's been looking forward to seeing us all day. "I'm having some sort of anesthesia tomorrow. Isn't that right, Dr. Benedict?"

"They were supposed to do that today," he says. His smile turns to a puzzled frown.

"Yes, but I drank a glass of water after they told me to flush dye from that magnetic test out of my brain," she says.

"Magnetic what?" I say.

"Magnetic Resonance Imaging scan," Gabriel says. "We looked at Mrs. Fritz's brain to make sure she didn't have a brain tumor or a stroke."

"Did she?" I say.

"Of course not, dearie," she rasps. "But what was so bad about drinking a glass of water?"

"They don't want you to throw up on the anesthesiologist," Gabriel says.

"Why don't they coordinate with each other?" I say.

"The entire medical system needs to be overhauled," he sighs.

Mrs. Fritz dozes off. I'm alarmed at how often and how quickly she falls asleep. Gabriel stands at the foot of her bed, picks up her chart. He studies graphs that, to me, look like a failed trigonometry test. I study the silver whales on the maroon tie he wears today.

"Have they figured out what's wrong?" I say.

He hesitates, looks toward Mrs. Fritz as if reluctant to awaken her or have her overhear. "Maybe we should go somewhere and talk," he whispers.

Mrs. Fritz wakes up as suddenly as she fell asleep.

I feel chaperoned. "I'm going down to the hospital cafeteria to have a cup of coffee with Dr. Benedict," I say, going to her side. "I'll be just a few minutes."

"Stay as long as he'll have you, dearie," she says.

The hospital cafeteria is crowded with worried clumps of

patients' relatives. Here, at Formica tables under fluorescent lights, eating is secondary to other preoccupations. Doctors and lab technicians in white coats hunch over their dinner trays, compartmentalized into meat, potatoes, vegetables. Gabriel nods at doctors and nurses who greet him in passing.

"I haven't eaten since breakfast," Gabriel says.

We take dinner trays and go through the cashier's line. I go first and pay for mine so Gabriel won't think I'm waiting for him to offer to. We hardly know each other and already our relationship seems overcomplicated by Mrs. Fritz's illness, my arrest, Gabriel's pending divorce, and this unexpected intimacy of having dinner together in a hospital, of all places.

"Why is Mrs. Fritz wearing that tape recorder?" I ask him when we find seats in a corner of the dining room.

"That's a Holter monitor," he says. "It's an ambulatory electrocardiogram, recording her heartbeats to be read by a computer. There are moments when her heart doesn't beat, others when it beats too fast."

Beepers go off all over the room, like panicked birds before a storm. I hear the clank of silverware, plates being scraped, chairs pushed back from tables. I worry about Mrs. Fritz upstairs, unable to touch her dinner.

"What can be done to fix it?" I say.

"We can't fix it, but we can bypass it, bring electricity directly to the heart muscle to make it beat regularly. We do it by putting a battery-powered computer under her skin on her upper chest."

"You mean a pacemaker?" I say.

"Exactly," he says, digging into his Salisbury steak, mashed potatoes, green beans.

He eats like a starved man, while I manage just a few bites of my spaghetti. It's stuck together, as if made hours ago. My peas and carrots taste like each other, from hours of sitting on a steam table.

"Do you eat here often?" I say.

"Every day," he says.

My heart aches to watch him eat such bad food with so much relish. He deserves three great meals a day. If I were his wife, I'd give him a bowl of oat bran granola smothered in yogurt and fresh fruit for breakfast, send him off with a sack lunch of thick sandwiches, cookies, and fruit juice. I'd have a hot dinner of real food ready for him when he came home.

"I'll make dinner for you sometime," I say.

He looks up from his plate, startled. His whole face lights up, surprised gratitude bursting through his studious concentration. "I'll take you up on that," he says.

He explains Mrs. Fritz's condition to me while he eats. I can't eat; I'm both worried and lovesick. When we're finished, he insists on carrying my tray as well as his to the cafeteria's disposal conveyor belt. I watch his empty tray, my practically full one, disappear down the hole to the dishwashers. Gabriel smiles at me, as if we're sharing a private joke. He's not smooth like Web, but he's genuine. His white-blond hair looks tousled from so much thinking and medical problem-solving. He's the sort of man who doesn't know he's good-looking. He probably goes to a barber instead of the kind of upscale unisex salon Web goes to for hair styling and mani-cures. Gabriel probably clips his own nails as matter-of-factly as he shines his shoes. In spite of my worry about Mrs. Fritz, my fear of what's going to happen to me, I feel a flash of happiness.

He escorts me to the elevator. The elevator door opens; we lean involuntarily toward each other, as if for a parting kiss. We catch ourselves. I'm swept up by the crowd getting on. He stands there as the door closes, gives me a little wave. I fly up, in the elevator's dizzying rush.

Next time my mother calls, I'll come right out and ask whether she wants me to come home. I'm the person the codependency books were written for, but codependency so permeates my being that I wouldn't have a self if it weren't my mother's. I'm thinking about this when Gabriel calls me at the library to tell me Mrs. Fritz has taken a sudden turn for the worse.

"Her cardiologist put in the pacemaker, but something's not right," he says, upset. "Colleen, I don't think she's going to make it."

He's sitting at Mrs. Fritz's bedside when I tear into her hospital room. She looks so wild-eyed and pale I hardly recognize her. I sink into the only other chair not covered with medical appliances, bedpans, white antiseptic-smelling towels.

Gabriel's eyes meet mine. He looks back at Mrs. Fritz, lifts her pale hand to place it in his. We wait and listen. There's an order to this listening, as if each of us must bring our concentration to bear on it. Her white eyelids quiver open.

"Are you in pain?" Gabriel asks her.

She gazes back at him. Her eyes grow brighter, as if she's glaring at something within herself.

"Where?" he says.

But the pain isn't ready to be spoken of, exposed. Sweat gleams on her high forehead. She shuts her eyes. We all back off, rest a moment.

Mrs. Fritz's roommate groans from her side of the partition. It suddenly occurs to me that my mother knows what happened to me in Galveston. But, of course, she doesn't. We're not even on the same wavelength.

"She could tell us she's in pain by moaning or something," Gabriel says.

Mrs. Fritz's eyes fly open; she fixes them on Gabriel. She opens her mouth as if to speak.

"Are you nauseous?" he says. He's at once cajoling and authoritative. His every gesture requests permission.

She turns her gaze to me. Our eyes lock.

Gabriel lifts the stethoscope around his neck and warms the metal cup in his hands. He reaches in and listens to her heart. "We need to find out what's bothering you so we can help," he says, his voice quiet and far away.

She and I could be dancing, eye to eye this way, she lying there with Gabriel's hands upon her. I want her to give up the reason that she hurts to me, so that I can give it to Gabriel as a gift. Love for him wells up in me like music. I offer it to her, barter for the secret of her pain.

Her face grows harder, the agony moving to the surface. It breaks on her face; her lips purse, her brow puckers. She mirrors my own misery. I'm sliding out of my life, evaporating. Why not keep going, slip over the edge? I'm melting from the inside out. My breath is a liquid, draining away. Tears collect in her eyes.

Gabriel leaves briefly to call Mrs. Fritz's cardiologist. I take the seat next to her bed. I put her hand, still warm from Gabriel's holding it, in mine.

"You'll—marry—him?" she gasps to me.

"Don't you think it's a bit—soon?" I say.

"I haven't got that much time," she rasps.

I don't know what to say, desperate to give her some good news instead of the grotesque chaos of myself. "I'll try—" I begin.

"Don't try, do it," she sighs. "I'll speak to him."

Somehow things have got out of hand. Gabriel reappears. He puts his hand on my shoulder, and I give him back his seat. He leans closer to hear what Mrs. Fritz is whispering to him, sits straight up again.

"You're both very sweet people," Mrs. Fritz gasps when I kiss her on her brow. It seems her Third Eye winks at me.

When Gabriel finds no pulse, no breath, he pinches the bridge of his nose.

That's when I know. I'm stunned to the point of immobility, stillness, silence. Gabriel goes out; I sit there for a while. Mrs. Fritz's roommate's television goes off for the first time. Even the building renovation ceases, down the hall. The silence seems flat, like a wall, but filled with metallic ripples of rumor. Sounds calculated to comfort, or madden? High windows humming with wind, a second hand sliding from second to second. The bony aristocracy of nurses arranges Mrs. Fritz in a sleep position. So much going on that she is not a part of. My own body breaks from me in sections. They take her away.

At the Lord's Motel, a spotlight shines down into the parking lot. My bedroom is never dark; it seems I've had a headache from this light for years. It shines through the trees as if the leaves are under scrutiny. The branches shake with a sinister rustle, the squirrels escaping from the cats. The cats squawl like babies. Everything is eating everything else.

11

U r b a n   A n i m a l s

A few nights after Mrs. Fritz has died, at dusk, St. Francis scatters her ashes on a small patch of grass behind the Lord's Motel. We're careful not to step on the brown cicada shells, intact but empty, in the grass. The cicadas molted, doubled in size to the green-winged bodies now roaring in the trees.

We're all here—Gigi, Barbara, the cats. I've invited Gabriel because I know Mrs. Fritz would have wanted him here. I'm having a hard time. It's as if I've been sad all my life and am just now realizing it. Mrs. Fritz meant a lot to me, but I didn't know how much. She was the one person I was sure wished me well.

"Gigi and I are having dinner at Kentucky Fried Chicken to honor Mrs. Fritz's memory," Barbara says. "Would y'all like to come?"

"I can't go anywhere they serve dead animals," St. Francis says. He goes inside to juice his avocados.

Gigi and Barbara go off, leaving Gabriel and me alone.

Pigeons are cooing in the parking lot. Such an undertone of cooing it's impossible to tell which one is doing it, until one of the males swells with pleasure, his throat feathers glistening purple and fuchsia in the late sun. He pads around his female, who at first refuses him. When he circles her again, she kisses the feathers of his throat and breast. He steps away, she hunkers down into a squat. He approaches her, he balances on her back. She spreads her tail feathers, in one swift movement he thrusts into her.

The world turns inside out. How am I supposed to feel, standing here with Gabriel, watching pigeons copulate near Mrs. Fritz's ashes?

"Why?" I say.

"It's always risky when we go doing things to ninety-five-year-old ladies," Gabriel says unhappily. "Most likely she had a cardiac arrest and nobody knows why. Maybe her pacemaker malfunctioned, or her cardiologist put it in wrong, or something else intervened."

We drive downtown to Edgar Allan Poe's, a dusky bar where the Urban Animals hang out. It's my idea, and Gabriel seems too depressed to protest. I wonder what he thought of Mrs. Fritz's last request, that we be together. Mrs. Fritz would have appreciated the punk, feisty fatalism of the Urban Animals. They're a roller-blading gang who skate the freeways wearing kneepads. Here they skate in, up to the bar, then zip around from table to table like killer bees checking out various flowers.

"Have you decided?" a waitress asks us. Even the wait-people are on skates.

"Decided what?" Gabriel says.

"Two Irish coffees, please," I say before Gabriel commits the faux pas of ordering a Perrier in here.

"But I'm on call," he says when the waitress skates away.

"The great thing about an Irish coffee is that it's an upper and a downer in the same drink," I say dolefully. "I use it to work on my equanimity."

"I feel this awful every time one of my patients dies," he says.

Mrs. Fritz would want us to start lightening up, get on with our lives. I worry that except for Mrs. Fritz's dying, Gabriel and I won't have anything to talk about. "Her dying doesn't mean you failed," I say.

"E.R. docs aren't supposed to get involved with patients," he says.

"I'm not your patient," I say.

"I mean, E.R. docs don't follow patients once they leave the E.R.," he says.

"Why did you do it for Mrs. Fritz?" I say.

"I was interested in her case," he says. "I was interested in *you.*"

"You were?" I say.

"I am," he says.

When our Irish coffees arrive I only want some of his. This could be a date if it weren't a wake. If I could get away with it, I'd slip my hand under his, wrapped around his cup. We'd touch. I'd kiss him off to the side of his face, start at the edge of his mouth and kiss up in a line toward his eyes.

He bows his beautiful head for several minutes, as if he's praying.

"Grace before Irish coffee?" I say.

"I was just thinking about my divorce," he says. "Death reminds me of it."

"I know what you mean," I say. It's a relief to be with someone who can get as depressed as I can. Web never takes anything seriously enough to get depressed. My getting arrested, Gabriel's divorce, Mrs. Fritz's death—it all goes together, somehow.

"In a way, divorce seems worse than dying," he says. His big hands grip his Irish coffee mug, but he hasn't sipped a drop. "At least when you die, you get to retire from public life."

When he says "die," I feel a lift-off, as if I'm picked up and moved through the air. Does Gabriel know how much I like him? I slurp the whipped cream off the top of my Irish coffee. Mrs. Fritz would be pleased I've got the conversation off dying and onto divorce, at least. "What's the worst thing about divorce?" I say.

Gabriel slides his whipped cream off with a straw and transfers it to my coffee. "My x-wife is fighting for custody of my son," he says. He puts the accent on the "x"—as in x-ray or x-rated.

"Will you get visitation?" I say.

"I hope so, but in the meantime she won't let me see him," he says miserably.

"What does your attorney say?" I say.

"He says we have to ride this out."

I'd never marry an attorney. "What's your son's name?" I say.

"Gabriel, Junior," he says. "Gabe, for short."

I picture a miniature version of Gabriel, two feet tall with blond hair and blue-gray eyes, wearing a little boy's clip-on whale tie.

"How old is he?" I say.

"Two," he says.

"Two?" I say.

"She says she might agree to a supervised visitation," he says.

"Supervised by whom?" I say.

"By someone known to both of us who's completely on her side," he says. "Trouble is, she can't find such a person."

The Urban Animals are like large children, flying in the face of tragedy. They pour out of the bar to join dozens of others, streams of them roller-blading past the windows. They're glorious in their pink and black outfits, silver skates, sequined kneepads and headdresses, blue and purple hair.

"Life won't always be this tragic," I say. "Lots of people get divorced."

"Have you ever been divorced?" he says.

"I've never been married; that's even worse," I say.

"Anyway, I don't really know what the problem is," he says, finally taking a sip of his Irish coffee. "My x-wife forced me to go to psychiatrists until we found one who said *I* was the problem."

"What's your x-wife's name?" I say.

"Felicity," he says.

"Felicity?" I say.

"You sound disappointed."

"It's just—it'd be easier if she were a Hildegard."

"I didn't marry her because she was a Felicity."

"How do you feel about her now?"

"Our marriage is a painful situation from which I'm trying to extricate myself," he says.

I want to hit Felicity, where what Gabriel has is high rage potential. He looks like a volcano waiting to blow, and when it does it will kill all the villagers. He wouldn't hit Felicity, and I'll bet his father never hit his mother.

"Have you treated battered women in the emergency room?" I say.

"Last night," he says. "She couldn't afford a plastic surgeon; she had only me to sew her up." He folds his arms, puts his head in them on the table.

My mother went into the hospital when I was ten, but at least she didn't die like Mrs. Fritz. I was afraid she would, and then my brother and I would have nobody. My father hit her one last time for leaving him. When she came home from the hospital, I was frightened because I didn't know how to take care of her. I listened carefully to the doctor's instructions. She cried when the doctor left. "Why are you crying, Mother?" I said. "The doctor said I was doing a good job, raising you kids by myself," she said. I can see now how that meant a lot to her.

"What are your parents like?" I ask Gabriel.

"My father's a rancher," he says. "Mother is just—Mother."

"How big is the ranch?" I say. "Where is it?"

"Just a few hundred square miles, west of San Antonio."

"You grew up on a ranch?" I say.

"Oh, no," he says. "We lived in town where my father could manage his business interests. The foreman and hands run the ranch. I'd have liked to go there on school vacations, but my mother always insisted we go to the Alps or Katmandu or someplace."

He takes a photo out of his wallet. It's a picture of him as an adolescent standing between two native South American Indians in front of a thatched hut. The man and woman have horizontal black stripes painted across their faces, bare arms, legs. The woman's breasts are striped; her feet and ankles are black with painted-on socks. They wear only skirts, striped red and purple and green. The man's hair is bright red as if dyed with berries, cut oddly around his head and plastered down. I wouldn't have thought the photo was taken in this century were it not that the man incongruously wears a watch, and that Gabriel is there between them. He's lanky in his Levis, already handsome at fifteen.

"This photo was taken in a village in Ecuador," he says. "I carry it around because this was where I first decided to become a physician." His smile seems to fall off his face. "The poverty and disease were unimaginable."

"Your parents must be so proud of you," I say.

"My father is," he says. "My mother wishes I were a plastic surgeon."

"But an emergency room doctor makes such a contribution to society," I say.

"My mother thinks a plastic surgeon makes a bigger contribution," he says. "Of course, she has a different notion of society."

"Does she ask you to come home for a visit?" I say.

"She *tells* me to come home," he says. "Sometimes I do, and sometimes I don't."

I'd pay him to let me love him. I can't bring myself to tell Gabriel what happened in Galveston. I'm falling in love with a man I'm too bad for. "I'm in a painful situation from which I'm trying to extricate myself, too," I say.

Worry works creases into his brow, beneath his thick blond hair. "I know Mrs. Fritz's death is very upsetting for you," he says, taking my hand in his.

In eighth grade, there were parties and the parents inexplicably permitted kissing games like Spin the Bottle. During the spinning—the hope of being kissed, the fear that someone would kiss you whom you did not wish to kiss, the terror that your beloved would kiss another. Gabriel kisses me with his eyes. He blesses me with a psychic kiss.

The horde of Urban Animals skates back into the bar again. Their blades clatter over the threshold, across the old wooden floor. For a second, I think I see Mrs. Fritz at the other end of the bar. Just her face in the sea of wild hair, pink and purple Lycra. Or her eyes, or a look—just an impression, maybe.

12

The Spider

It's pouring, one of those tropical rains Houston has. I drive to work through the Fourth Ward, my VW in first gear to rush slowly through the lakes in the street. My mechanic told me to do this, to keep water out of the engine by exhaust. On flooding days in the ghetto, the curb outside one house or another is piled high with furniture. Were the sofas and chairs soaked through, ruined by roof leaks? Or were the people just evicted? There's the feel of the eternal to it, all of it, my driving through, their presence. I feel them, but I can't find my way through to what they're feeling, thinking.

Suddenly, my VW bug falls into a huge sinkhole—a soggy spot where the street just collapses. I sink in slow motion as the street gives way beneath me. The car drops a foot to a spongy stop. I sit there, terrified to get out of my car in the middle of the ghetto.

Then I'm lifted up, lopsided at first. Three black men, two in the back and one in the front, lift my bug out of the sinkhole. They place it down gently on the street.

"Thank you so much," I say, rolling down my window, but they're already heading back to the sagging porch they were

ting on. One of them turns around to grin at me. I start
my stalled car and drive off.

Walking through the administrative halls of the library to
a meeting with Joanne, I'm sure everyone can tell I've been
arrested. Where do I fit now into Houston's Southern bureaucracy, from the suits and boots at the top to the vast masses
of baffled paper-shufflers below? Probably on some mezzanine
of mediocrity, staffed by middle-management hatchet men
who terrorize pools of chubby secretaries into never being
late for work.

"Colleen, do you think you can relieve all the suffering in
Houston?" Joanne says when I tell her I want to add my
emergency room component to Service-to-the-Unserved.

I want to do it as sort of a memorial to Mrs. Fritz. "Maybe
not all of it," I say.

"I'm in favor of expanded user statistics," she huffs. "But
you're not going to pick up any new readers in an emergency
room, for Christmas sake."

"If you were on your way to the hospital in an emergency,
would you remember to bring a book from home?" I say.

"I suppose not," she says.

"They don't know they're going to be there for six hours
at the very least," I say. "In that time we could make them
library users forever."

User statistics line up in her eyes like pictures in a slot
machine. "One of our Trustees is also on the Board of the
Hospital District," she wheezes. "I'll see that you get clearance."

"Thanks, Joanne," I say.

"March straight down the hall and tell the Public Relations
Team exactly what you are doing," she says.

"Yes'm," I say. That's Southern for go jump in a bayou.

I sneak back down the hall instead, ducking my head so

that no one will nab me for some tedious discussion about some bit of information I have that he needs to move his own mountain of paperwork a little bit forward. The administrative air is thick with everyone else's projects and questions. Outside my office, in the photocopying room or the staff lounge, my object is to hold my own projects in my head so when I see someone I can ask one of my questions before he asks one of his and makes me forget all my own. It's like trying to pick up glitter with boxing gloves on.

Dragging the canvas library bags through the stacks, I select Dolores's art and vocational books. I select from the various classifications for the other inmates, but what use have they for books on etiquette, interior decorating, cooking? They can't garden or watch stars.

Dolores isn't wearing her glasses when I meet her this time in the jail lobby. Her face seems naked; she looks younger, more vulnerable.

"You got contact lenses!" I say. "They're much more becoming."

"No," she says, looking at me as if I'm crazy. "Some creep stole my glasses."

"In jail?" I say.

"Everything happens out there, happens in here, except worse," she says. "Ain't nothing *but* criminals in here."

"Of what use are your glasses to someone else?" I say.

She shrugs. "If they can't see with them, maybe they can sell them. Maybe they want to use the glass to cut somebody."

"When will you get new glasses?" I say.

"I'm, like, on the waiting list," she says, in a flat tone. The waiting list is probably years long.

Lieutenant Sprunt comes out of his office. He saunters over to our side of the lobby as if he has something to tell me. What if the criminal justice system computer has told him I've been arrested? "Well, now. I got a room in the jail for you," he says, watching for my reaction.

My blood runs cold. "For me?" I say.

"You'll still give the books to Dolores in the lobby," he says, "but the inmates can pick them up and return them in the library room."

With relief I realize he means a room in the jail for the inmates to use as a library. I've been asking for one for months; he always said no. It was predictable, the way Web used to ask me to marry him and I always refused. "May I see it?" I say. In my mind I'm already outlining the article I'll write for *Library Journal*.

Lieutenant Sprunt frowns at me as if I'm endlessly demanding, but he sighs and unlocks the door from the lobby into the jail. Dolores and I look at each other in surprise. We follow him down the gray concrete corridors, Dolores pushing the heavy book cart as if it's Sisyphus's stone in Hades. We pass through gate after gate as Sprunt unlocks and locks them behind us, each clang punctuating the din. The shouts of men in one section, of women in another, echo off metal bars and walls. It sounds like a cavernous zoo, a nightmare of animals, wounded and starving. How does Dolores stand it? I look furtively at her; her face is impassive.

Lieutenant Sprunt gets paged just as he unlocks the door to the small, bare room that will be the library. He locks us in, then scurries away. The room is chill with gray, unpainted cinderblocks. Dolores and I stand there, looking around. There's not much to look at.

"This is a closet," I say.

She shrugs.

"We'll have to ask for some shelves," I say. "And a table and some chairs." I pace the tiny space, trying to figure out where furniture would fit. I try to visualize it, but I'm oppressed by the clammy room, the dank odor of despair. The entire jail smells like that, a mix of sweat and mildew. It reminds me of my elementary school basement, where we were herded down for air raid drills. We huddled there in terror, sure that the schoolyard was being blown up, that our homes were being bombed to smithereens and we'd never see our parents again. Finally we were brought back up and expected to go back to our lessons as if nothing had happened.

Dolores unloads the books from the book cart onto the concrete floor. I help her, putting the vocational books she requested in a separate pile—cosmetology manuals, books on hair care and manicures.

"Dolores," I say, handing her a stack of art books, "I thought you might like these on different techniques."

"Techniques?" she says, squinting at them.

"Yes," I say. "Still life, foreshortening, perspective, figure anatomy, portraits, seascapes."

She squints harder. "Can't read them, my eyes are too bad," she says.

"Could someone read them to you?" I say. "Do you have a friend in jail?"

She thinks about this for a minute. "Just you," she says.

I'm so touched, I don't know what to say. We stand there nervously, waiting for Lieutenant Sprunt to come back and let us out. Dolores seems embarrassed, as if she's being held hostess.

"You must feel trapped in jail," I say.

"It's bad, but not like living with my husband, him beating up on me," she says.

"You didn't leave him?" I say, stunned.

"Where could I go? What could I do? I asked myself over and over," she says. "Where could I go with three kids? I got so I was afraid to move. He came home, I didn't know what kind of mood he'd be in, I was trying to make everything okay."

"Didn't your parents or somebody try to help you?" I say.

"I was afraid to ask them—they told me before I married him he was no good. But I was sixteen, I wouldn't listen, I wanted to get out of the house. I was pregnant so I dropped out of high school and we had our three kids, one after the other. I had made my bed and had to lay in it."

She had made her bed and had to lay in it. I think of my parents' bed, and Web's bed, the water bed in the Honeymoon Suite, the beds nailed to the walls in the Galveston jail cell.

"Did you have a job?" I say. "Did you try to save money so you could escape?"

"*He* was no good at keeping a job, for sure," she says. "He was always out drinking. When my kids were old enough to be left alone, I got a job cleaning at a health club."

"A health club?"

"Where they do aerobic dancing in strange outfits," she says. "I washed their towels and scrubbed the showers. But my husband came on Fridays when I got paid and took my money. I was afraid he'd pick a fight and I'd lose my job."

Learned helplessness. That's what the books said about battered women. They were too shocked to object, and if they did, they got flattened. "How old are your kids now?" I say. "Where are they?"

Her face goes doughy, collapses, pushing down the corners of her mouth. My mother's face looked like that when she was trying not to cry. Dolores even turns the same strange color of dough, a kind of beige—soft and bloodless. "Billy's pumping gas, he stays at his girlfriend's. He's eighteen," she says. "Grace, she's seventeen, living with my mother, trying to finish high school. My oldest, Johnny, he's nineteen, in jail for armed robbery."

"In *this* jail?" I say.

"I never see him, though," she cries. "He's on the men's side."

How awful for her, not to be able to look after her children, not to know how they are. "Do the other two visit you?" I say.

"Gracie does, once in a while," she says. "She's a good girl. Billy's a good boy, he just don't like to think about me in here, I guess. Then, his brother's here, and they don't get on."

I feel woozy and claustrophobic, my skin tingles with fear. I walk over to the door and stare out the small barred window. I hear the clatter of gates, see inmates sauntering up and down the hall. "When does Lieutenant Sprunt plan to let us out of here?" I say.

"You better stay out of sight," Dolores says.

"I should?" I say.

"Some of the inmates are always looking for a way to make trouble," Dolores says. "You look scared. If they see you, they might try to take you for a hostage...." She shrugs.

Terrified, I step away from the window. "It's just that I'm a little claustrophobic," I say. "I'm afraid to be in places I can't get out of."

"Jail would be a bad place for you," she says.

"You're telling me," I say, rattling on in fear. "I spent a night in jail for doing something my boyfriend put me up to. If I get convicted I could go to jail for a year."

Dolores's eyes widen in horror. "He was a bad influence on you," she says.

"My mother was abused, like you," I say. "She had kids and no money so it was hard to get out. But I had no excuse for what I did, I was just stupid."

"We all feel like we was stupid," she says. "We can see, now, what we would have done different."

I was already in love with Web by the time he asked me

to do those things. It was easier to do them than to fall out of love with him. "Did you love your husband?" I say.

"Sure," she says. "At first, anyway. Then I loved him in between the times he beat me. It felt like, in between, I needed him to love me even more. I loved him and I hated him. Even after this was going on so long I couldn't feel nothing, I could remember what I used to love about him."

Web kept me off-balance like that, alternately upsetting and calming me. He flirted with other women to make me feel insecure, used me to act out his sexual conflicts. Then he'd give me presents, tell me how much he needed me. While he was calming me down, I forgot he was the one who had upset me in the first place.

"Lieutenant Sprunt left us here on purpose, didn't he," I say, fighting my panic.

"He doesn't know you're afraid of being locked in places," she reasons. "He maybe got busy and forgot."

I learned by heart the patterns of abuse my mother tried so desperately not to teach me. "How did you finally get away from your husband?" I say.

"I killed him," she says.

"You killed him?" I say.

"That's why I'm here," she says.

A spider lowers itself into the space between Dolores and me. Its small black body rolls into a ball, its tiny legs working an invisible thread.

"How did it happen?" I say, so softly my breath doesn't even disturb the spider.

"He'd been trying to pick a fight since supper, then to force me to have sex," she says. " 'Ready to turn in?' he said, shoving me, not very nice. He knew I was afraid. He busted my mouth, then he pushed me into the bedroom. His pistol that he kept in the drawer by the bed? I picked it up. He lunged at me and I shot him. I meant to *stop* him—I didn't mean to kill him." She wipes a tear from the corner of her eye with the tip of her little finger.

"Then it was self-defense," I say.

"I'm still awaiting trial," she says. "I got no money to post bond."

She has so little that she reminds me of one of those plants that lives on air. She's dispirited, the way I became in my love-life with Web. Dispirited—that was it, except for brief moments of inspiration that seemed about to rise, phoenixlike, from the ashes of our corruption.

"What did your kids say, when their father died?" I say.

"Gracie and Billy, I think they was relieved," she says. "Johnny said, 'Ma, just tell me he hurt you that bad, you had to do it.' "

"I'll bring you some law books," I say, helplessly. "Now that you can read at a higher level."

"I can't read them without my glasses," she says.

We hear Lieutenant Sprunt jangle his keys on the other side of the door. The spider rises as mysteriously as it descended. We don't see the thin, retracting filament, just the tiny being floating upwards.

13

Bearing Expert Witness

Chisholm Jim counts money while I tell him my tale of woe. He's supposed to be the best defense attorney in Texas for this type of litigation. Maybe more librarians are arrested for prostitution than I thought.

I sit on a red leather chair in his office in a magnificently restored old house on lower Westheimer. It's as if a River Oaks mansion were picked up and moved to the middle of the demimonde. "I office where my people are," he said, giving me directions over the phone. The house is furnished with antiques and exotica from all over the world—persian rugs, Ming jars, tapestries, oil portraits, mahogany tables with claw feet. He has one of those sliding ladders to reach the antiquarian first editions in the bookcases stacked to the ceiling. *La Traviata* pours out of his CD player.

Chisholm Jim himself looks like a rancher in a china shop. His silk repp tie lies crisply on his one-hundred-percent cotton shirt, wrinkled from roping steers. His cowboy hat has left a dent in his bushy brown hair.

I don't understand how he can count money, thousands of dollars in large and small bills, and listen to me at the same time. He's like one of those psychiatrists who leans back in his chair to gaze out the window while you unload your entire unconscious.

"We'll take care of it," he says, rising when he has finished counting, putting on his hat. He's dismissing me already and it wasn't even my money he was counting.

"But...but—" I say. What is he, some kind of Wizard of Oz with a stable of paralegals he'll terrorize into solving the case?

He raises his bushy eyebrows.

"Don't I want to ask you some questions?" I say. "I mean, don't you want to ask me some questions?"

"You tell me," he says.

I stare at his Mickey Mouse watch. He puts his hand over it and I wasn't even trying to see what time it was upside down.

"What's going to happen to me?" I squeak finally. "What's the punishment for prostitution?"

"Awww, Class B misdemeanor?" he says. "Up to no more than a year in jail. Fine, maybe." He looks around like he's looking for some more money to count.

"I could lose my job," I say.

"Could," he says. "But this is maybe a defensible case."

"What will be my defense or whatever you call it?" I say.

"Little of this, little of that," he says. "No offer and accept-ance, maybe duress."

"No offer and acceptance of *what*?" I say.

"Money, of course," he says. "It's not prostitution if you didn't take money for it."

"But didn't I just get through telling you I did take money for it?" I say.

He rolls his eyes. "The prosecution has to prove that," he says.

"You mean I should lie on the stand?" I say. "You want me to *perjure* myself?"

"I didn't say that," he says.

This conversation is going backwards. Web told me if I ever get audited, I should answer only the questions the auditor asks and not volunteer another word. Web gets audited every year and he always wins in a blazing triumph of gray areas.

"What I took money for wasn't prostitution," I say, standing up and wringing my hands. "Who's going to believe I took all that money for half-dressed conversation? I wasn't even naked until I peeled off my wet lingerie."

"Awww, if he conned you into doing it as a fantasy and the guys gave you a little tip afterwards, theoretically there was never an offer to engage or agreement to engage, it was sort of an afterthought," he says. "'Course, that would be the defense—now, whether a jury would buy that would be another story."

"Jury?" I say. "I was hoping not to attract that much attention. I'm not an exhibitionist by nature."

"Even if we go to trial this won't attract much attention, unless the media get all excited about it," he says.

"Can we please not make this a media event?" I say, wincing at the thought of the library Public Relations Team giving new meaning to "Service-to-the-Unserved."

"Now, we could have a trial before a jury or just before a judge," he says. "If we draw a court with a fair-minded judge who's had a jillion prosecution cases come in front of him and he knows a bullshit case when one comes around, we're better off there than with an unknown jury. On the other hand, if we got a hard-ass judge with a big stand on law and order, we'd be better off with a jury."

"Can we avoid any kind of trial altogether?" I say.

"If we plea it, we might get rid of it real quick," he says.

"Plea it?" I say.

"Plea bargain, plead guilty, maybe to a lesser charge. 'Course, with a conviction for a crime of moral turpitude, you can never be bonded, never serve on a jury, never hold public office, never go to law school or medical school, you couldn't do lots of things."

"I don't want to go to law school," I say. "What kind of lesser charge could we get?"

"Just because you were standing there naked with a bunch of money in itself is not a crime," he says. "It may be public lewdness or indecent exposure. Now if you were acting out your fantasies outside in the azalea bushes it'd be a different story. Being busted in that hotel room could present a problem but that's where we'd use the duress."

"What do you mean by duress?" I say.

"You did it for your boyfriend, didn't you?" he says. "You were afraid if you didn't do it he'd do something to you."

"What was I afraid he'd do to me?" I say.

Chisholm Jim lifts his cowboy hat to get some air in under there. I feel the warm Texas breeze blow across the range.

"The psychiatrist will tell you that," he says.

"What psychiatrist?" I say.

"Our expert witness," he says. He's losing patience with me. "You're not that different from a battered wife."

This thought makes me feel as faint as church used to. I sit back down on the leather chair. "Will Web come for the trial?" I say.

"Where is he?" he says.

"On a cruise, or at a Club Med in Bangladesh or someplace," I say.

"We're talking misdemeanor," he says. "We can't extradite Mr. Wrong back for that."

Mr. Wrong. Web is someone I love, fear, am addicted to, codependent with, and have to get away from permanently. A hush falls over the antiques.

"So he set you up, then he split," Chisholm Jim says, shaking his head. "A lot of juries would be offended by that. It's like my little transies—they got a bee in their bonnets that the vice officers hustling them on the street wouldn't kiss them. So they tell the officer, 'Okay, you gotta kiss me.'" He laughs ruefully. "Then those motherfuckers kiss them and bust them."

"Transies?" I say.

"Bless their hearts," he says, "I represent a bunch of transvestites. The cops humiliate them. The transies still got their danglers, but they go out and spend money for boob jobs, nose jobs, chin jobs. They still dangle, and anytime the cops see them on the street, they pop them. What they do, they make them pull up their blouses and they play with their tits. They bring all the other cops around and they're doing this shit. Makes me so damn mad, half the time I represent 'em for free."

I wish I could give him some money to count. "What's your fee for my case?" I say.

"What do you want?" he says. "You want probation, you want to plea, you want to fight?"

"I want the whole problem to just go away," I say. "How much for that?"

"The bureaucratic nature of the D.A.'s office, there's so many checks and balances now, they're afraid to dismiss a case even if it ought to be," he says. "Most prostitution cases aren't handled by the chief but by one of the little baby prosecutors. Everybody ought to go to jail, in their opinion. For me to go in and say, 'Hey, this is not a prostitution case, this was a tip for a good time,' the baby prosecutor'd go 'Aw bull-*shit*.'"

"So what will it cost?" I say.

"Case like this," he says, lifting his hat again. "Awww, run you about seventy-five hundred."

"Dollars?" I say. "Do I get a refund if we lose and I go to jail?"

He laughs. "I got to talk to that vice cop who busted you to see if the prosecutor can offer evidence you had knowledge of any offer to engage," he says. "All we got to do is plant a reasonable doubt."

I've never felt more dubious in my life.

"Miss Colleen," Chisholm Jim says, sitting down again, "don't confuse moral guilt with legal guilt. If we convicted everybody on morals, we'd *all* be in jail. Legally, this is not a prostitution case. Morally, you're guilty, more likely than not. We could get some little D.A. who's morally outraged that a librarian would do this, and he'd have a hard-on saying he's going to make sure you're convicted. He'd stay with this case and make damn *sure* you're convicted so none of our little Southern Baptist children get influenced by this liberal prostitute librarian. He's going to send you off to jail, make an example of you to all the wayward librarians in the world. We got to outfox him, skin him without his knowing he's been skinned. Talk to the judge, maybe, over whiskey. Now, I can't tell the judge anything we can't prove." He swings his boots with their pointy toes up on his desk, leans back in his chair.

I try not to look legally guilty. "What if someone's guilty legally but not morally?" I say, thinking of Dolores. I doubt she's getting seventy-five-hundred dollars' worth of counsel from her court-appointed lawyer.

"Prosecutors don't think in those terms," he says, crossing one big boot over the other. He looks like a Wild West sheriff sitting on a saloon's front porch. "They see a dead body, they see the smoking gun, they see the person with the smoking gun, that's all they need. They don't have to prove a motive, all they have to prove is she pulled the trigger. That's their case, they win."

"What would happen to a battered woman in jail awaiting trial for murdering her batterer?" I say.

"A court-appointed lawyer would start talking plea-bargain, most likely. Five to ninety-nine or life. She'd end up pleading out for a murder that by all rights she shouldn't."

"Why someone did something is so important," I say.

"Aww, I don't really give a shit why you did this," he says, leaning forward. "I see a good story we could sell to the jury. There's enough truth to the defense that you were under Mr. Wrong's influence, that you can testify truthfully that's why you did what you didn't do."

Chisholm Jim's secretary suddenly shrieks from her office.

"What's the problem, Annette?" Chisholm Jim calls out.

"I just got off the phone with the autopsy info for that woman who was murdered?" Annette says. "In the list of her clothes they said she was wearing Sears panties! Can you imagine being caught dead in Sears panties?"

"Lord, no!" Chisholm Jim says, and winks at me.

"She was killed in her brand-new red Mustang convertible," Annette goes on. "Better she'd been wearing no panties."

"There you go," Chisholm Jim says. "That was her trade-off, Sears panties for a red Mustang. She had *her* life in order." He sits back and looks at me.

I try to remember whether I'm wearing Sears panties. I came in wearing my guilt like a shawl, and the more he talked the more it unraveled. Except instead of my guilt going away, I'm now sitting here wearing this totally unraveled shawl.

"Little lady," Chisholm Jim says, "you worry about your moral guilt and leave the legal guilt to me."

•

Why does our city always smell as if it's burning? It's not your city, and it's you who smells of burning, I think as I drive at six the next morning to the office of Dr. Smythe, the psychiatrist Chisholm Jim says will be our expert witness. I have to see him before work. If the Public Relations Team found out, they'd pick it up and run with it.

No one's out on the streets until I turn onto Westheimer, still raw with its own night. Last night the whores came out; as the day blackened the lights glittered on. People crowded the bars and restaurants. The discos grew louder, the street-lights glowed orange. Cars cruised by the massage parlors and oriental modeling studios, picking up curb service. In the tattoo parlors, customers waited their turns; crackheads and dealers met on the corners. Those who couldn't find what they came for grew drunk and desperate, bought cheaper whores, staggered down the street. The night sank on its side.

It feels like Lent. At six in the morning, still half-asleep, we sixth-graders sang the daily Requiems for the parish dead. Sister Immaculata, tiny and furious, conducted us with her arthritic hands.

Now, boy whores with long blond hair and curvy asses walk home to their pay-by-the-week motels. I stop at a red light. One man follows another out of an all-night Circle K, hoping for a swig from a quart of Coke; the other wipes his mouth and leans against the wall. Used-up women on their way to work smoke and wait for the bus. This end of the night is bright with metallic light. Everyone is wary but too tired to hurt someone else.

I drive through this bad neighborhood to get to Dr. Smythe's office in a good part of town, the Museum district. I press the coded digits on his office door and open it. No receptionist in sight, but Indian bells on a silken strand on the door ring to let someone know I'm here.

The paper collages on the walls are tactile under glass. On the coffee table, *Town and Country, The New Yorker, Architectural Digest.* I try to decide which one I'd want to be caught reading. My heart beats too quickly in the burnished waiting room, as soft and red as the interior of a heart. It's a little after the time for my appointment and I still haven't seen the doctor or his receptionist. Maybe they're having sex on his couch.

The door to the inner office opens, and a man in his fifties comes to me with hand outstretched. "I'm Colleen Sweeney," he says. "You're Dr. Smythe."

He doesn't correct his Freudian slip so I don't know if this is a joke or what. Before Freud, nobody understood anything, and now that we do, we're even more miserable. Dr. Smythe holds the door open for me and I pass through. I was hoping for someone short and pudgy, but Dr. Smythe is tall, British, unforgivably handsome. I prepare myself to resist positive transference, employ my distrust of attractive men. They're arrogant; they should be allowed to take us places but not to win our hearts.

His sofa and chairs are tan leather. It's an intimate room— warm, male, cozy but not too. I look at a wall of framed diplomas. There are hundreds of them, big ones. I size up the chair situation. I know the importance of selecting a chair.

"Sit here," he says.

He doesn't want to confuse me or, should I say, add to my confusion. But I'm not confused, just excruciatingly self-conscious. I read Dr. Smythe's clothes for social cues while he reads mine. He looks too comfortable in his blue shirt, brown and blue tweed jacket, to have relied excessively on his wife's taste. His tie has no whales on it, but it seems to me a phallic object and I refuse to look at it. He sits down and stretches out his long legs.

I feel the weight of it, the impossibility of telling someone you've never met before enough so he can help you. Everything I do or say, the way I reach for a tissue or glance at him or place one word after another, will reveal everything. But not at first—first the welter of disguises, then everything else in fifty minutes. I'm exhausted, thinking of the effort it'll take us.

Dr. Smythe puts the palms of his hands together. He's either praying or diving.

"I'm the librarian charged with prostitution," I say, wondering what Chisholm Jim has told him. "I didn't go through with it, it just *looks* like it."

"Ah," he says, as if he's used to this. It's the short, intellectual "Ah" educated people use when someone's explaining something to them—a difficult piece of music, Russian Constructivism, things like that. His "Ah" is a nice counterpoint to Chisholm Jim's Southern drawled "Awww." He nods at me, then closes his eyes.

"Where shall I begin?" I say.

"At the beginning, of course," he says, barely rousing himself to answer.

Any story of myself includes wars, fires, famines. My essential experience of myself is one of horror. I tell Dr. Smythe everything about the Sexcitement with Web. Dancing for Foster and Gillian, my costumes, the bachelor party.

"Tell me, why did you dance at the bachelor party?" he says, perking up when I get to that part.

"Web wanted me to," I say.

"Why did you do what he wanted?" Dr. Smythe says.

I did it for Web, but Web didn't make me do it. How can

I explain this to Dr. Smythe? "I was trying to find the connection between love and sex," I say, weakly.

"Ah," he says, studying me as if he might admit me to a locked ward this very morning. "Tell me this, then. Why did you go up to the Honeymoon Suite with the groom and his ushers?"

"The dancing wasn't enough for Web," I say. "He wanted more. I talked to the guys in the bedroom one at a time, but I couldn't go through with the prostitution."

"You did this—au naturel?" he says.

"I wasn't naked until I took off my wet lingerie, right before the vice officer showed up," I say. Why do I always seem to be explaining this to someone, including myself? "Why does this seem as if it happened to someone else?"

"You're defended against it," Dr. Smythe says.

"Defended?" I say. The best and the worst feelings don't seem that different from one another after a certain point of intensity. We have only so much capacity, and the straining of that capacity is what we feel, not the goodness or the badness of the feeling.

"You're afraid you'll overload your emotional computer," he says. "If you brought it up into consciousness all at once, you could lose functionality."

I could lose functionality. I visualize my computer terminal at the library, the way the monitor screen goes crazy with a blizzard of terrifying symbols whenever I hit the wrong key. "Ah," I say.

Dr. Smythe is taken aback. "How did you come to look for love in all the wrong pieces?" he says.

"I've failed to see the connection between love and sex all my life," I say. "I don't recall my parents showing even affection for each other."

"Of course you fail to see it," he says. "Your parents didn't 'model' it." Dr. Smythe says "model" as if it's in quotes. A lot of what he says, in fact, sounds as if he's quoting it.

"But other people 'model' it," I say. "Why do I feel, when it comes to love, I have to reinvent the wheel?"

"The wheel has been invented, but everyone has to make his own," he says.

Am I afraid I have to invent my own wheel before I can make it? It's not what happens to you, it's who you become while it's happening. I created a self, moment to moment, out of bits of string, twigs, flint. Then I forgot who I was.

"Web kept me off-balance by flirting with other women," I say. "He'd come back to me just when I felt I'd lost him."

"Why did you put up with it?" he says.

"He persuaded me that my own feelings were irrelevant," I say. "He said I was at my best half-naked and could make so many people happy."

"You never put your foot down?" he says.

"He said my anger was unreasonable, my response out of proportion. Then I wound up apologizing for both my anger and my response."

"Ah," Dr. Smythe says, sinking into himself again. He's quiet for a while. "Your feelings are valid just because you have them," he says finally. "Now, what you do with those feelings is something else."

I'm stunned. This whirls around in my mind the way I whirled in my black feathers for the men at the bachelor party. "Why do I always feel there's something wrong with *me* when someone else treats me badly?" I say.

"There *is* something wrong with you," Dr. Smythe says.

"What?" I say.

"We're going to find that out," he says.

This doesn't reassure me. I try to remember what it felt like, in the beginning, to do what Web asked. Something in my life made me feel like a shoplifter being watched by a moving camera in a store. The only relief for it was actually to do something wrong. Dancing for Foster and Gillian seemed oddly innocent, not sinister the way unremitting self-judgment is, unacknowledged feelings projected anonymously through a camera in a discount store.

"I wanted Web to *love* me," I say.

Dr. Smythe raises his eyebrows, as if trying to make them hold his eyelids open. Is his sleepiness the ultimate in non-directive psychotherapy? Maybe he's practicing avoidance, or maybe I'm just boring.

"It wasn't just the kinky sex," I say, battling my way through my confusion. "At heart, that wasn't the problem."

"What was it?" he says sleepily.

I don't want him to fall asleep; I want him to stay awake and listen to me. I want to find the right answer, the real reason I did those things. "He didn't force me to do anything, he set me up," I cry. "He made me feel that I had to do something special—something other women wouldn't do—to be *loved*." It's a familiar feeling; it goes all the way back to—what?

Dr. Smythe's sleepiness has the feel of parental neglect. My body breaks into a sweat. I'm dying, like Mrs. Fritz. I look out the window next to my chair, to the trees swaying in the early morning breeze. Could I slip out the window when Dr. Smythe falls asleep? A green lizard on the windowsill molts, its skin white, translucent. I crawl out of mine and walk away. In the leaves, the naked lizard glows a brighter green.

I'm so depressed. Maybe I should ask Dr. Smythe to pre-scribe antidepressants, except I heard they make a person gain weight. No matter how happy they made me, I'd still be depressed if I were fat.

"Wake up!" I say to Dr. Smythe. "Do you think I should try antidepressants?"

"They work fine for the people they work for, and not for the people they don't work for," he says, coming to.

I look at him blankly. "If I'm dangerously depressed for more than a week, I have a cup of caffeinated coffee," I confess.

It's his turn to look blank.

"I know I shouldn't use it like a drug," I say. "But I get desperate sometimes."

"It would be all right if you had a cup of coffee *every day*," he says. He looks as if he could use a cup of coffee. He closes his eyes.

I meditate with him. Are these the myths we create for ourselves, and is this how we create them? When was I last so distant from myself? Taken all together, are we the divine presence who came here and forgot? Somewhere there's someone who's free to love, to be love itself, who doesn't condemn any of us. He stirs as our fifty-minute hour is ending. It seems to me that God himself is stirring.

"That's the whole story," I say.

"Ah, I see," he says.

14

D i n n e r

One Friday evening after work, I stop to buy groceries, then rush home to the Lord's Motel. I'm cooking dinner for Gabriel, as promised. St. Francis, Gigi, and Barbara stand in the parking lot, watching roofers rip off our roof. The Lord's Motel has needed a new roof for a year; why did the building owners send roofers today?

"Roofers are like welders," St. Francis says to Barbara.

"St. Francis!" I say, before Barbara can reply. She's eight months pregnant and huge. She looks ready to deliver any minute and I wonder if she might—right here in the parking lot—to terrorize St. Francis.

"I thought I didn't have to worry about you anymore either," St. Francis says to me.

"I'm not perfect yet," I say.

"God will do anything to get your attention," he says.

St. Francis thinks my anxiety is a sign I'm somehow not conforming to the will of God. Quarts of dandelion root tea and herbal diuretics haven't made a dent in my grief for Mrs. Fritz or my terror that I'm going to jail. Not to mention that

I'm still crushed that Web could abandon me so easily; at the same time I'm worried sick he'll reappear. "God's not trying to punish me with terminal PMS," I say, a wave of anger nearly knocking me down. "Maybe he's trying to do me some kind of weird favor."

"PMS?!" Gigi says, giving me a look. "Think of what we have to look forward to—osteoporosis, arteriosclerosis. Depending on estrogen after menopause, we have a choice between cancer and heart disease."

"*Lung* cancer," St. Francis says to her.

"Don't be so hard on us," Barbara says to St. Francis. "We're not over losing Mrs. Fritz, especially Colleen."

"The good Lord gives and the good Lord takes away, and usually when he takes away it's to give you something you don't have room for yet," he says pointedly to me. "What's in your bag?"

"Groceries—I'm cooking dinner tonight for Gabriel," I say.

"I eat from memory," St. Francis says, looking into the bag. "I don't taste anymore, it's just sensation."

"Sensation?" I say. "The second chakra?"

"Sweet, sour, or chocolate," he says. "What are you cooking?"

"Shrimp Pernod."

"How much Pernod does it call for?" He pulls the bottle out of the bag.

"A few drops, but I'm hoping to make him Shrimp Pernod for the rest of my life."

Gigi and Barbara give me supportive looks.

"Praise God," St. Francis says, dubiously.

I go upstairs, sit at my kitchen table, and devein shrimp. The roofers bang over my head. I hope they're gone by the time Gabriel gets here. I start the water for the linguine. I heat olive oil, sauté onions and celery. I simmer tomatoes in the sauce, add herbs and spices, squeeze lemons. I set the table with my two china plates, two place settings of flatware. Beside myself that Gabriel's coming for dinner, I get my polish and shakily do my nails.

Gabriel knocks on my door; the roofers' hammering stops. All I hear is my pounding heart as I look out at him through the peephole.

He holds up his driver's license. "Hello, darlin'," he says.

We ease our way into each other's presence. I memorize him, then give him the wet-nail-polish hug. You have to put your back into it since you can't use your hands. It reminds me of one of those sex positions with the woman's legs straight up in the air.

"You give the best hugs," he says.

He's growing a beard. Blond and coarse, it makes him look like an angelic lumberjack. I stare at it, speechless, taking in his entire, wonderful face. I'm stupefied with happiness.

"Do you like it?" he says.

"I do," I say.

He has brought chilled champagne. We sit in the living room, sip champagne, and eat caviar on little toasts while my nails dry. I look down at my nails; they look polished by Jackson Pollock. I desperately want this to be a romantic evening. I ricochet back and forth between excitement and nervousness, unable to tell them apart.

"I like your apartment," Gabriel says. "It's bright and airy, but also soft and serene."

"Thank you," I say, glad I turned down the lights to a rosy glow. My palms cast leafy shadows on the walls. "What's your apartment like?"

"It's okay," he says, "but it's not—decorated, like this."

"Not decorated?" I say. I've never thought of my apartment as decorated. It's just a collection of things—Art Deco furniture, mementos, books—accumulated over the years. I wish I could see it through Gabriel's eyes. I'd like to see myself through Gabriel's eyes, deep with tender interest.

"You'll have to come see it soon," he says.

"I'd like to," I say. I'd like to get up and go there right now. Then I remember I've got him here at *my* apartment.

"How was your day at the library?" he says.

I can't remember a thing about it. "Fine," I say. "What sort of day did you have? Did you save a lot of lives?"

"A few," he says, with a smile. "This is the first chance I've had to sit down."

His beeper goes off. I toss the salad and listen to him talk on the phone. His voice softens me, makes me vulnerable to the word of love spoken by every being in the world at every moment. I hear the roofers finally drive away.

"How do you stand it?" I say when we sit down together again. "The emergency room."

"It's just trying to help people and working within a bureaucracy," he says. "My x-wife saw these as character defects."

"How could she?" I say.

"I'm sure I didn't spend enough time at home with her," he says, downcast. "And when I was with her, I was probably preoccupied with my patients in the emergency room."

Would Gabriel be as emotionally inaccessible as Web, for different reasons? "I can see where that would be a problem," I say. In any case, I admire Gabriel's candor.

"I'm working on it," he says. "I'm trying to get straight with myself, so I can balance my work and my personal life. It's even more critical now, now that I have a son."

"Has she let you see your little boy?" I say.

"Not yet," he says, picking up an empty set of plastic juice can yokes from my kitchen counter. He takes out his Swiss army knife and starts cutting apart the plastic rings.

"What are you doing?" I say.

"Seabirds get their necks stuck in these when they show up in the ocean as dumped waste," he says.

It's hard to cheer up a man going through a divorce. I love the man he'd be if he weren't so disconsolate. His beeper goes off again. He jumps up; I get up to sizzle the shrimp in my sauce. I eavesdrop over the roar of the cicadas outside the kitchen window, listen to him prescribe generically— medicines shot through with white, fuchsia, aquamarine. Diagnosing, reassuring, he's answering prayers. He ministers to his patients, we all minister to one another. What is our love but a nexus of lovers?

"I really love your beeper," I say, when he sits down at the dinner table. I light two tall white candles.

"Beeper fascination is a stage interns go through, before that gives way to the resident's resignation and the physician's chagrin," he says, giving me a gentle hug as I serve him his Shrimp Pernod. "I'm going to love your Shrimp Pernod."

I blush. May his appreciation for my cooking never give way to the fiancé's resignation and the husband's chagrin. "To the beeper," I say, raising my glass. Maybe he didn't spend enough time with his wife, but what a difference there is between a man you can page on his beeper and one who's always off on a cruise.

He raises his flute but looks unsure of what we're toasting. I look down and get a facial in the steam rising from my Shrimp Pernod. We wait, suspended like that, for a few moments. The world fans out around us. A kiss, made of flowers, hangs between us. I sound his heart; his trust rests like a kiss on my soul. How could Felicity let him go?

"If you're working on your relationship problems, why are you getting divorced?" I say.

"Felicity wants to look for someone with values that more closely approximate hers," he says. "That's part of it."

"What kind of values?" I say.

"Richer doctor, bigger house," he says.

"Really?" I say. He's already as rich as I could handle.

"I love my work in the E.R.," he says desperately.

"I love your work too. What would have happened to Mrs. Fritz if you hadn't been in the emergency room?" Then I remember she died. "What's the other part of it?" I say.

He considers this, an expression of pain on his face. "I failed," he says finally. "In some basic way, I failed." He looks at me as if I can tell him why.

I'm bowled over now by his honesty, not just with himself, but with me.

"What's Felicity like?" I say.

"Having a permanent fit."

"What makes her angry?" I say.

"I spent six years trying to figure that out," he says. "She woke up angry, she went to bed outraged."

"I can understand that," I say. "Sometimes I wake up crying and can't stop all day."

"She got angry enough to file for a divorce, furious when I tried to work things out, livid when I agreed to the divorce, and now she's determined to make me pay for all those enraged years she had with me."

"She couldn't have been angry all the time," I say.

"It was always there, waiting to blow," he says. "I was

tense during the good times, knowing it would hit the fan any moment."

"You were a battered husband," I say. "Emotionally, anyway." At least Gabriel didn't shoot Felicity.

He looks down at his dinner. Worried that I've reminded him too much of his unhappiness, I watch him eat. He endears himself to me with every bite. I know somehow that something is going to happen between us, but it's still unmanifest. It's like knowing the moon is in the sky but having to wait for night to see it. I used to think it was a sign my love was genuine if I wanted the man to wind up with the best woman for him, whether it was me or not. Now I don't care who Gabriel winds up with, as long as it's me.

"I have a lot of faults," Gabriel says. "My attorney says that anyone who likes me the way I am now wouldn't be good for me."

"That's certainly true of me," I say. "I'm bad for everybody."

"What I mean is, I wouldn't be good for *you*," he says.

In spite of what he says, he's humming with a kind of high energy. We're infinitely private, safe in a glass bubble of each other's quiet. I'm fragile and precious; he's carrying me from one place to another. A high order of events is unfolding exactly as it should.

"No?" I say. "But even when you're bad, you're good."

He smiles with relief. I savor his face. Absorbed in gratitude, he endears himself even further to me. I can hardly believe the affection in his blue eyes. He leans over to kiss me. I lean toward him, afraid to believe this is happening. His kiss is eager, hungry, warm on his manly lips, warm on mine. We fall together into the kind of kiss you go into not knowing what to expect, even though you'd imagined it a thousand times, and once into it, want never to come out again. We kiss and kiss, a continuous wave of questions and answers. Always the same question, always the same answer— yes, yes, yes.

When it's over, I lean back, startled. My blue necklace catches on the fork I still hold mid-air; it bursts into my pasta. The beads turn the noodles blue. Gabriel jumps up and starts picking beads out of my dinner, like a surgeon removing bullets. He wraps my wet beads in his napkin.

I clear the dishes to recover my composure. Over strawberry shortcake and coffee, I give Gabriel the Adopt-a-Whale packet I sent away for.

He tears open the sealed envelope with his whale's name certificate and a list of sightings. " 'Apollo,' " he reads. " 'Named after the god of the sun, prophecy, and medicine. Last sighted in nineteen eighty-nine.' "

"In nineteen eighty-nine?" I say, aghast. "We'll get you a different one, you can't adopt a dead whale."

"We don't know that he's dead," he says.

"Not sighted since nineteen eighty-nine?" I say. "You don't call that dead?"

But Gabriel's already attached to this whale. "He's deep in the ocean, thinking things over," he says. "He'll be back, you'll see." He eats his dessert with as much thoughtful appreciation as he did his dinner. Then he gets up, lies down slowly on my floor. He stretches out like a beached whale.

My heart pounds and sputters, like a tide coming in on short waves, then long. As if so much is happening out at sea it can't make up its mind when it reaches shore. "After your divorce, then what?" I say after a while.

"I have no idea what comes next," he says.

I stare at him, through his gloom. It's hard to find him in the fog of it. "I know what you mean," I say, and stretch out beside him.

"They'd have called us clinically depressed in my psychology rotation," he says, staring up at the ceiling.

"I'm not depressed, I've just had enough of life," I say. "When you're depressed you can still think of something that'd cheer you up if you could get it, but I can't think of a single thing."

"Thanks for adopting me a whale," he says, and rolls his head sideways toward me. I want to roll over onto him, but that might betray his trust. He trusts me enough to lie down on my floor. If we were married, would I check his trousers pockets on my way to the dry cleaners and find out he's having an affair? He's trustworthy, but can I learn to love someone I trust?

He looks into my eyes. I decompose layer after layer of prepared expressions. I look into his. "What do you see?" I say.

"Bewildered love," he says, stroking my hair.

He draws me to him, into his warm smell of emergency room elixir—a mix of musk and Mercurochrome. He's streaked with darkness. Lying heavily against his chest, I'm filled with danger. With his hand, he begins to create a woman of such pain and love that only a man with equal pain could love her.

Suddenly, I find myself telling Gabriel all about my arrest in Galveston. I tell him about my exotic dancing, my costume of feathers and plumes. I get swept up in it, absorbed in the telling as if describing a nightmare, fascinated by the bizarre imagery of it. I frantically hum a little of the disco music. "Then the disco music stopped; the men stampeded toward me. They didn't look human," I cry. I describe my terror, try to put it all in chronological order, to make sense of all the pieces coming up. " 'Why should I do this?' I said to Web; 'Why do you do anything?' he said," I say, doing both of our voices, then the parts of the men in the wedding party—the groom about to marry a librarian, the asexual best man, the suffocation freak, the usher so fat he broke the water bed. It all has a feeling of unreality, something that could happen only in a recess of the mind so deep as to harm nobody.

Gabriel stares, transfixed, at me. His face is impassive, cool. I worry that he's as bored as if I *were* recounting a dream. I tell him how the vice officer handcuffed me while reciting my rights as if they were the Twenty-third Psalm. " 'The Lord is my shepherd,' " I say, then describe my ride in the police car along Galveston's seawall. Then my mug shots and fingerprinting, the other women in my cell. Gabriel looks stunned by my story, his eyes glazed with horror. He has withdrawn, gone someplace I can't follow. He's silent for several minutes.

"So what do you think?" I say hesitantly, when I can't stand the tension another second.

"What am I supposed to think?" he says. He sounds hurt and angry, confused.

What did I expect, that he'd feel sorry for me, show the compassion he feels for his patients? But I'm not his patient. "It's not as if I murdered someone," I say, frightened.

"You should have," he says. "Aren't you angry at Web and those guys?"

"I went along with them," I say. "It's not as if I didn't have a choice."

"That's even worse," he says, his voice shaking.

This is the kind of story you should never tell anyone; they don't want to know you have all of this inside you. They don't want to think they have it too, they don't want to be infected with it. "You think I'm terrible," I say. "You think I'm a—"

"It's not that," he says, cutting me off. "I don't know what to think. I don't understand how you can talk about it so calmly, as if it happened to somebody else."

His voice is weighted with anguish, but I feel rebuked. Darkness smolders inside me. I've thrown a hand grenade into my own place of darkness, to make myself move out of it.

A few minutes later, he gets up and leaves.

15

Mother

The first thing I always notice when I get off the airplane at Boston's Logan Airport is that people are all bundled up. At Houston's Intercontinental it's always the faint smell of mildew. I know I'm at La Guardia when people are wearing black, and at Miami's airport when everyone's speaking Spanish. At Chicago's O'Hare they're also bundled up, but not in L.L. Bean, the way they are in Boston.

My mother is waiting for me on the other side of the electronic detector. We slant toward each other, hugging at the shoulders. Not at all like a Unitarian hug, the moral alternative to adultery. Her shoulders seem lower than before, as if her purse is pulling her down. Her face seems more translucent, her silver hair shorter.

"Let me carry your purse, dear," she says while I struggle with my luggage.

We find her car, inch toward the Sumner Tunnel, eight lanes of traffic merging into two.

"Let me pay the toll," I say, but before she left home she put the dollar on the dashboard.

We crawl through the tunnel, under Boston Harbor.

"Did you run into much traffic on the way in?" I say.

"Not too much," she says.

"I should have taken a cab," I say.

"Most of the cab drivers don't speak English," she says.

"They don't have to speak English to drive," I say. I'm sorry the second I say it.

She doesn't respond, grips the steering wheel, stares straight ahead. We're stuck in the tunnel, breathing exhaust. We break through, finally, into the dusk. Dusk in Boston is always brown, the burnished brown of copper, brownstones. I chatter about my job, my apartment, my friends; these grow trivial in her silence. The sun goes down over the expressway. The way to her house is suburban and complicated. We drive up her street, hilly and tree-lined. She moved to her white clapboard house from the housing project after Doug and I left for college. It's home to me, but not really.

"Stand back, dear," she says as she turns the key in her door.

Humphrey, her enormous golden retriever, throws himself with a thud against the other side of the door.

"What is *wrong* with that dog?" I say.

"He's just happy we're home," she says.

Humphrey plants his front paws on my mother's shoulders. He and I scuffle; I protect myself with my suitcase while he whacks me in the legs with his tail.

"He's not as lively as he used to be, his arthritis has slowed him down," my mother says. "But I'll distract him while you take your suitcase upstairs."

I fight my way up and slam the door. My mother aired this old room in the attic, under the eaves. The breeze blows out of the sky, across the wallpaper flowers. The white cotton curtains billow like clouds. She dusted the cherrywood dresser, starched the dresser scarf, made the bed with fresh sheets, fluffed the pillow. She filled a vase with zinnias and daisies, polished the wood floor until it glowed in the light of the old porcelain lamp.

"Mother," I say when I go back down, pointing to the pantyhose snagged on the heel of her shoe.

"Oh my God," she says. "I take off my slacks and my pantyhose together, then when I put the slacks on I forget the pantyhose are still in them."

Humphrey looks plaintive, sprawled in front of the refrigerator.

"Why's he looking like that?" I say.

"He wants some ice cream," she says.

Humphrey raises his ear flaps.

"Not until you've had your dinner," she tells him.

His ears collapse again.

"What are we having?" I say, getting up to stir it on the stove.

"That's Humphrey's beef stew," she says. "Our casserole is in the microwave."

We're setting the table together when the microwave beeps and she drops all the silverware. She has the Irish terror of small appliances—pressure cookers, doughnut fryers sputtering with grease, electric frying pans, blenders, hair dryers. You touch them with hands wet from the dishwater, they attract lightning, they blow up in your hands.

We sit down to dinner, a macaroni and cheese casserole with peas. My mother and I always sit at her dining room table, never in the kitchen. It's in keeping with the formality of our relationship. It's as if I'm here to do someone else's job, but I don't know whose or what the job is. I wait for my mother to tell me, but she expects me already to know. I could ask her, but she wouldn't know what I was talking about, and I'd feel even more inadequate than I do now. It's a little humiliating.

"This is a great casserole," I say.

"I lost the recipe," she says.

I'm homesick even though I'm right here. I'm a doll at my mother's tea party. I worry that she feels the awkwardness. I can take it, but I worry that she can't. I'm tougher than she is. "You're a fighter, like your father," she once told me. "Your brother hates fighting, like me." This had a devastating effect on me at the time. I had taken it for granted I was like my mother and her side of the family. To be like my father was to be diabolical.

And really, my father did nothing to dispel this. Even when he stopped drinking, his other unhappy characterisics revealed themselves. With his compulsive talking, his constant posturing as the great guy he really wants to be, it's as if he never stops shadowboxing with himself. I won't see him this visit, because this bothers me even more than my mother's silence.

After dinner, I clear the dining room table, load the dishes into the dishwasher. Before my mother had a dishwasher, in the project, she cut her finger on a knife while washing dishes. She wrapped it in a dishtowel and drove to the emergency room. She took me with her, she wanted me there. Her hands shook on the steering wheel. Now I think that what my mother meant by fighter was survivor. Or should have meant, when applying it to me. What does it mean to *survive,* and is she doing it? She depends on the kindness of strangers like me.

Humphrey paces back and forth behind me, his toenails clicking on the kitchen linoleum.

"That dog is getting on my nerves," I say.

While I'm shaking the tablecloth out the back door, my mother surreptitiously rearranges the plates I've placed in the dishwasher.

"Just tell me what was wrong with the way I did it," I say, "and I'll do it your way next time."

"The china breaks if the pieces touch," she says. She puts her kitchen sponge in with the plates.

"You wash your kitchen sponge in the dishwasher?" I say.

"How do you wash yours?"

"In the washing machine," I say.

"Some people don't even wash their sponges," she says.

How can I have so much now, when we had so little then? In the vacuum between my mother and me, there's a world of mothers and children. She sang "Twinkle, Twinkle, Little Star" to my brother and me. She drew us pictures of cats and trees. She created what order she could for us, in our schedule of homework and baths. Saturday afternoons in the summer, she lay in her folding chair on a small patch of project dust. I stretched out on a folding chair beside her, but I couldn't understand how she could just lie there, in the sun. "What do you think about?" I said. "Nothing," she said.

She walks around the house now, watering her plants with her teakettle. I take Humphrey for a walk around the block with his Pooper-Scooper, while my mother vacuums.

She's vacuuming with a vengeance, almost fuming, when I get back, as if vacuuming is what life is all about. "Someone called while you were out," she shouts over the roar of the vacuum cleaner.

"Who was it?" I holler back.

"Gabriel somebody," she says.

"Gabriel?" I say, my heart speeding up.

The vacuum sucks up the rug fringe with a bup-bup-bup sound. My mother tugs frantically at it. I hold the rug down with one foot and shut off the vacuum cleaner.

"What sort of mother would name a boy Gabriel?" she says.

"Maybe he's named after the archangel," I say. "What's wrong with that?"

"An archangel!" she says. "Why couldn't she just name him after a saint if she wanted to be religious about it?"

I seriously doubt Gabriel's mother was spiritually motivated. "It's just a bit unusual, Mother," I sigh.

"Talk about unusual," she says. "He had the strangest foreign accent."

"That's Texan," I say.

She considers this, looking longingly at her vacuum cleaner. She'd love to turn it on again, but she wants to continue our heart-to-heart, such as it is. I wish I could explain that beyond the Massachusetts borders, Chicagoans speak with a flat "a," South Carolingians with verandah gentility, and Texans with a drawled anarchy undreamed of by her.

"Does Gabriel say 'shucks,'?" she says finally.

"Of course not," I say.

"Then this person wasn't your Gabriel, because he said 'shucks,' " she says. "I'm quite certain of it."

I try to remember whether I've ever heard Gabriel say "shucks." I probably have, actually; it just never struck me as the hick word it does my mother. "How did the conversation go, exactly?" I say, exasperated.

" 'Hello?' I said," she says.

"Yes?" I say.

" 'Hello,' he said. 'This is Gabriel Benedict. May I please speak with Colleen?' " she says.

"Yes!" I say.

" 'Colleen's not here at the moment,' I said," she says.

"No," I say ruefully.

" 'Well, *shucks*,' he said," my mother says with smug disapprobation.

I myself am overjoyed that Gabriel would say "shucks" because he couldn't talk to me. It means he was disappointed, but I see the image of Gabriel forming in my mother's mind.

A bowlegged cowpoke in chaps and a flannel shirt, his leathery face working a chew of tobacco. "He's a *doctor,* Mother," I say.

My mother adjusts her mental image to a bowlegged cowpoke in a white doctor's coat, his leathery face working a chew of tobacco. "Well, be that as it may," she says.

"Texas has more doctors than cowboys, Mother," I say. "It has a lot of educated people."

"Yes, but they were educated in Texas schools," she says.

"Texas schools aren't any worse than schools elsewhere," I say. "And Texans go to colleges from the east coast to California."

"California doesn't count," she says.

I'm not about to defend California when I'm up to my neck defending Texas. "You underestimate Texas," I say. "They have paved roads, French wine, cable TV."

"I know that, dear," she says, sliding the silent vacuum cleaner back and forth. "I'm not ignorant."

"Texans aren't ignorant, either," I say, "just because they say 'shucks.' "

"Promise me you'll never say 'shucks,' " she says.

"Jesus," I say.

My mother looks shocked. "You weren't like this before you went to Texas," she says. "And whatever happened to that Web I liked so much?"

I brought Web home once for Bunker Hill Day, a big holiday in my family. One of the first major battles of the American Revolution was fought near Bunker Hill in Boston, on June 17, 1775. The British won, but suffered heavier losses than the Americans. Web didn't know Bunker Hill Day from Halloween, but he was charming and attentive to my mother. Web is the sort of man mothers like. I don't know why it matters to me *what* my mother thinks. My mother is already suspicious of Gabriel, and she hasn't even met him. "Web wasn't all he was cracked up to be, behind that altar-boy face," I say.

"At least he was from Connecticut," she says.

"Jesus," I say, again.

"The nuns didn't teach you to say that," she says.

"The nuns didn't teach me a lot of things I need to know in life," I say.

My mother unplugs the vacuum cleaner, starts coiling up the cord. Why do I so often feel I've hurt my mother's feelings? She's the last person in the world I'd want to hurt. I've spent so much of my life feeling powerless to protect her from my father. It's excruciating how loving my mother hurts. I watch her put away the vacuum cleaner, drag it into the closet, hide it behind the winter coats. She's not really provincial; she wants to feel safe but she can't. I don't want to be like her; I want to go back to Texas.

I call Gabriel back, but he doesn't answer. His answering machine is broken—it won't accept my message.

My mother and I sit together in the living room, at opposite ends of the sofa. We read, drink, and share a box of crackers between us. I read a book on prison libraries; she reads a mystery. She sips a very dry martini; I sip a cold glass of chardonnay. It's just like it was when I was ten, except she drank beer and I drank ginger ale. I even gave her a beer mug then for Christmas.

Humphrey lumbers over.

"His arthritis gets worse in the evening," my mother says.

It's painful to watch Humphrey drag his arthritic self up onto the sofa. I wish I could help him but I don't know how to push a dog up from behind. Once up on the sofa, he turns around and around to find the right spot. He can't decide which end of him my mother and I should get. He sighs and snuggles his head into my mother's lap.

"Heads you win, tails I lose," I say. I shrink up against the arm of the sofa to get away from Humphrey's ass.

"He likes you, dear," my mother says.

"You used to be a cat person," I say. "How did you get to be a dog person?"

"People change," she says.

I'm wearing out on the notion of blaming my parents. It's not that they didn't have any input, but I had to get *through* that to realize that who I am doesn't have that much to do with them after all.

Sometimes, instead of reading, my mother and I watched TV.

"Do you still watch TV, Mother?" I say.

"No," she says. "Late-night TV has those horrible commercials for nine-hundred numbers now. 'Girls, Girls, Girls,' they say. 'Hot, Hot, Hot.'" My mother looks unhappy, as if she wants me to tell her those girls don't really exist.

I feel the urge to protect her at the same time I'm angry at her naiveté. Did I think by acting out Web's fantasies I could prove to him there were no ghosts in his nightmares? Or not to try to be perfect anymore, to be swept up by it, to give myself over to it, my heart sinking. Did shame so obscure our pleasure that we could have no pleasure without shame?

"Where's their self-esteem?" she goes on, bewildered.

When I think of self-esteem, I think of Moderately Priced Dresses. Of my mother and me, when I was a girl, taking our baths on Saturday morning and going in town. We took the bus to Harvard Square, went down into the subway, waited on the platform. The station was cool, dark, damp; it smelled of scuffed dirt and the piss of old men. I breathed shallowly like my mother, standing beside me in her cherry-red coat from Filene's Basement. She held her mouth tightly. We never sat on public toilet seats or breathed deeply in the subway.

The train screamed in. The voice of our fear curled around the ceiling of the tunnel, vibrated up the platform, up our hipbones to our lungs. In the echo of the roar I watched my mother's lips move; she pulled on my coatsleeve and we passed through the train's sliding doors. In the press of the crowd we avoided men's bodies.

I sat beside my mother, her knees rounded in her nylons. Women who shopped in Moderately Priced Dresses called them "nylons," women who shopped in Better Dresses called them "hosiery." My mother pulled her red coat over her knees and we folded our arms over our purses in our laps. We read the train ads, Preparation H and correspondence courses and Office Temporaries, stared over the heads of cheap girls and slouching boys from East Cambridge, who poked each other and smoked. Because I wasn't cheap like them, my mother would buy me nylons and a garter belt to wear to Mass. We'd go to Woolworth's so I could buy a pink lipstick with my babysitting money. I daydreamed about my lipstick while the train burst from the tunnel. We saw the Charles River out the window, the boathouse, boys crewing.

Harvard, Central, Kendall, Charles Street, Park Street—we got off at Washington Street so we could walk through the turnstile directly into Filene's Basement. We averted our eyes from the panhandlers, the skinny, stubbled men who made the subway smell. Everything that they were, we were not. We were poor but clean. The Better Dresses ladies took the elevator to the Beauty Salon on the Mezzanine, but we rode the escalator. I hung on to the moving rubber railing, gazed down into the filmy garden of Intimate Apparel.

"There are all kinds of people in the world," I say lamely.

My mother gets a strange, unhappy look on her face. It's

uncomfortably familiar: I'm reminded suddenly of Dolores. My mother wants to tell me something. Is it what I've waited so long to hear?

"Like your father," my mother says, finally. "I'm sorry I gave you kids such a rotten father."

I feel a sudden, murderous rage toward my father.

Humphrey gets up. He's so arthritic that his front legs won't hold his huge bulk as he slides off the sofa. He collapses onto his face. He lies there for a moment, looking sad. I feel awful for him. I've never seen that happen to a dog before.

My mother sees my horror. "He does that all the time," she says.

I can't tell whether this means she feels worse than I do, or is just used to it. It must be heartbreaking to live with a dog like Humphrey. He laboriously picks himself up. I try to figure out whether he's embarrassed or just resigned. Is it codependent to worry how a dog feels? He limps off to my mother's bedroom.

That's why I don't have an animal—I couldn't bear to see it in any kind of pain. There are so many things that can't be fixed—so many things, once done, no one can do anything about. I'd feel so helpless I just couldn't stand it.

That night, Humphrey drags himself up the stairs to my room to breathe sadly in my face. I drift in and out of a bad dream that Web comes back. When I can't stand it anymore, I drag Humphrey out by his collar and shut the door.

He cries. He misses me hopelessly, the way I miss Gabriel.

"Humphrey!" my mother says, getting up to scold him from the bottom of the stairs. "She doesn't want you in there."

I get up and throw open the door. "He can come in if he wants to, it's just that it's not going to solve anything for him," I say.

I doze off and on the rest of the night, waking from time to time to Humphrey's sad whimpering, his big head on his front paws. Even humans make that screeing sound, of tears in the throat. It's a constricted feeling, the heart squeezed almost beyond endurance.

Early the next morning I hear the paper girl open the storm door and drop the newspaper with a thud. Humphrey barks hysterically. You'd think he'd get used to the paper being delivered day in, day out, year after year. Because I stay in bed later than my mother, Humphrey thinks I'm dead. He worries, he cries and licks my hand. He trudges up and down the stairs until my mother comes to see what's the matter. He marvels when I resurrect myself, waving my arms to prove it.

When I go downstairs, my mother is reading the paper and drinking coffee while Humphrey pads about disconsolately. I rummage in the kitchen cabinets for some cereal and sit down at the other placemat. I spoon sugar from the plastic sugar bowl I gave my mother when I was a child. The little white sugar bowl fills me with an odd happiness. I spent hours choosing it, standing in front of the housewares shelf at the A & P. "A sugar bowl?" the girls at school laughed. "That's not a present." But it was a present, because my father had broken my mother's sugar bowl.

I try again to return Gabriel's phone call. He's not there, but his answering machine works this time. At the tone, I leave my name and phone number.

My mother does the crossword puzzle, while I read the other sections of the *Boston Globe*. The local news doesn't seem so bad since it's not local to me. The national news, on the other hand, looks worse this far from Texas. The international news bodes planetary chaos.

The phone rings. It has just got to be Gabriel.

My mother answers it. "Hello?" she says. She listens, then

puts the receiver on the floor. She calls Humphrey to the phone. He barks into it for several moments.

"It's one of those computerized sales pitches," my mother says, seeing the shock on my face. "I wait until the beep for name and phone number, then I let Humphrey split their eardrums."

Why hasn't Gabriel called me back? Did my message sound too desperate, or too cavalier? Why does leaving a message on Gabriel's machine send me into paroxysms of self-doubt? Web has dropped out of the picture because he doesn't care what happens to me. It would be too much if Gabriel dropped me too.

My mother and I spend the day quietly, puttering, snacking, reading. When it's time for her to drive me back to Logan Airport, she can't decide which route to take. We sit in her car while she weighs the disadvantages of the Southeast Expressway, the Massachusetts Turnpike, even Route 128 part way to pick up one of the others. Not to mention the different ways to get to these. Boston was built before anyone heard of urban planning.

"Some of those ways must be less roundabout than the others," I say. "Let me look at a map."

"No," she says.

For her, the best route has nothing to do with geography. It has to do with traffic, time of day, weather, potholes, bad neighborhoods versus long, solitary stretches of back roads. We go the way we came when she picked me up, mostly because I remember it. It starts to snow. Her tires leave dark tracks on the white road. It's early February, still wintry enough for a blizzard.

"Did you hear a weather report?" I say.

"The weathermen all disagree with each other," she says. "*They* don't know."

The snow drives down harder. My mother's defroster can't keep up with the haze on the windshield. She concentrates nervously on the slippery road. I'm frozen with fear that she'll skid on the ride home alone. She and I turn love into worry, worry into love. I collude in her worry, to ward off the terrible things hurtling toward us from the dark depths of the sky. It's as if by recognizing them from far off, we might soften their coming. As if we might soften their destruction.

We slide along the expressway, out of the Christmas-card woods of the suburbs. Snow covers the roofs of East Boston's three-decker houses, of the historic brick buildings downtown. We take refuge in the fluorescence of the tunnel, until we emerge at the airport. My mother drops me off, anxious that I catch my plane, anxious to turn around and start back home. We want to say we love each other, but our feelings run too deep.

"Well, 'bye, Mother," I say.

" 'Bye, dear," she says.

Blue lights, Noxzema-bottle blue, border the airport runway. They guide the jet in the swirling, white snow. My mother still has some winter to go, but February in Houston is early spring. All along the Azalea Trail, the varieties will be starting to bloom. Delicate Pink Pearl, brilliant Flame Creeper, King's White, Southern Charm.

16

Prison Fashion

Chisholm Jim is trying to keep me out of Hell by getting me into Purgatory.

"When can we get this over with?" I plead, calling him from my office.

"I want you to prepare yourself, it may take four or five court settings for us to get to trial," he says. "You're going to feel like nothing's happening. I've already identified the legal issues. I can't advance them for you until I get a jury in the box. Now, you can sit around and work yourself into a high state of excitement, and bounce off the walls if you want to, but that ain't going to change one thing. Showtime doesn't start until the curtain draws. The curtain doesn't draw until the jury's in the box, and I may not get the jury in the box for months from now."

He pauses. I have nothing to say for myself.

"We're in a holding pattern," he goes on. "Aww, if you're going to sit and freak out and call me every week and try to figure out what's going on, you're going to be real frustrated, because I'm going to tell you, there's nothing going on. I promise you the prosecutor doesn't even know your name, you're a *cause* number. You're like somebody at the morgue, you got a number and that's all you are to them. You're just another prostitution case."

I hide in my office, worrying about my prostitution charges, worrying about Dolores, still grieving for Mrs. Fritz, and now kicking myself for destroying my fragile relationship with Gabriel. I hope Web doesn't reappear while I'm feeling so vulnerable. I can't bring myself to implement the new emergency room component of my Service-to-the-Unserved proposal. What if I run into Gabriel in the emergency waiting room? He'd think I was throwing myself at him.

Joanne wants to talk to me, but it's not about the emergency room component. "Your proposal for a jail fashion show won Most Original Non-Print Project in the American Library Association contest," she gloats when I tiptoe into her office.

"Surely you jest," I say. I'd forgotten all about it. I wrote it months ago under the delusion that a makeover and new clothes would help Dolores. Gigi told me then it was silly, and she was right.

"It kills so many birds with one stone," Joanne goes on. "We'll get so much publicity that even the conservative Trustees will act like liberals. The library once again takes the lead in community relations!"

By the time I get to the jail with the unfortunate news of the fashion show proposal, the library Public Relations Team has beat me to it. They've set up our meeting with Ms. Merry, an image consultant, then run off to wreak havoc elsewhere. That's the way they operate; there's no one to argue with about their irremediable arrangements.

"This is the worst thing that ever happened to me," Lieutenant Sprunt says. He's waiting for Ms. Merry as eagerly as if she were a lethal injection.

Dolores looks more pale and drawn than usual, but she's psyched about an image of the Blessed Mother on the floor of the jail lobby. The inmates see it, the corrections officers see it, everyone except Lieutenant Sprunt sees it. There *is* a dark area on the damp concrete, but to me it looks more like a Rorschach blot.

"I wrote the fashion show proposal months ago, before I knew better," I say, returning to the problem at hand.

"Look," Lieutenant Sprunt says, "I'm under a federal court order here for overcrowding. They got me monitored for non-compliance in staff ratio, medical care, segregation of pre-trial detainees, you name it. The only thing I got compliance for is underwear policy and library books. What kind of compliance am I going to get for a damn *fashion show?*"

"I'll have to derail the Public Relations Team, but how?" I say.

"The Constitution protects prisoners from cruel and unusual punishment," he moans.

"Good, we can use that," I say. "I'll write a counterproposal. What's the goal of punishment?"

"To reinforce society's values," he says.

"But what if society's values are worse than the inmates'?" Dolores says.

We both turn and look at her. She shrugs.

"Maybe they won't riot so they won't get blood on their new clothes," Lieutenant Sprunt says glumly, and storms off when Ms. Merry arrives.

Ms. Merry looks the way she probably did as a cheerleader twenty years ago; she's the only one who won't have changed a bit at her high school reunion. With her big green eyes and perfect blond hair, she reminds me of Suzi, my aerobics teacher—another one of those hyper-perky women on a coffee high all the time. They stay up all night orchestrating their wardrobes, giving themselves facials, starting on their makeup while the rest of us are sleeping. They're uniformly enthusiastic about everything, from man on the moon to a new line of pantyhose. "I want to affirm our commitment to providing you with better quality contemporary clothing," Ms. Merry gushes to Dolores. "Our designers strongly believe that finer fabrics and workmanship maintain a better garment look over time, resulting in a happier prisoner."

"Some of us are doing a *lot* of time," Dolores says.

"We want to become familiar with your fashion require-ments so we'll be able to continue to serve your needs," she says. "You wouldn't want to be paroled only to find that no one's wearing what you wore before you were convicted."

"Most of what I wanted I got because I was wearing the right clothes," I confess.

"What will you wear for the fashion show?" Ms. Merry asks me. "Obviously you're a Summer."

"I've been color-analyzed and I'm a Winter," I say. "I'll wear sackcloth and ashes."

"I *love* it," she says. "*Women's Wear Daily* will die."

"What am I?" Dolores says.

"*You're* the Winter," she says. "The new collections are being designed with lots of stripes as a tie-in to the jail market, but you should stick to vibrant solids."

"Stripes went out of style for prisoners ages ago," I say.

"Let's get started on your makeovers," she says, ignoring this. She unpacks her supplies; it reminds me of Arts and Crafts at Brownies. Maybe if I do my hair blond I'll get enlightened.

"I'd like to be made over in the Image of God," Dolores says. She's taking the vision of the Blessed Mother on the floor of the jail lobby more seriously than I could have imagined.

"Take off all your makeup," Ms. Merry says.

Dolores isn't wearing any makeup, but Ms. Merry snaps "Before" pictures of us when I've peeled off mine.

"That's mean," I say.

"Your body is your canvas," she says. "In the first thirty seconds, the other person makes eleven assumptions about how much money you have, how intelligent you are, and how moral."

"How moral?" I say.

"If your Person Image Profile is slut," she says, "people are going to think you are, whether you are or not."

"If I'm part of the mind of God, why do I have to wear makeup?" Dolores says.

How can I make a new body to inhabit, out of leaves, powder, lipstick, stones, all glued together with nail polish? I'm the first to be color-coded. Everything Ms. Merry tells me is the opposite of what I was told the last time I was color-coded.

"Are these carpet remnants?" I say, when she drapes me in swatches—reds, purples, emerald, black, turning them like the pages of a book.

"You should wear everything with a blue undertone," she says. "Earthtones—never!"

"This is very illuminating," I say.

"Did you say humiliating?" Dolores whispers.

We reassemble our faces piece-by-piece with computer-assisted, state-of-the-art skin care analysis.

"You must, must, *must* exfoliate," Ms. Merry tells us.

We wipe away our dead, real skin and put on fake—foundation, contouring cream, blusher, eye shadow.

"If you have this body type," Ms. Merry says showing us a glossy of one of the four basic fashion personalities, "you must wear shoulder pads even in your pajamas. The pitfall for the Romantic is looking like a little girl. The Natural can look underdressed, the Dramatic overdressed, and the Classic just plain boring."

"I feel worse than before she started," Dolores whispers to me.

"You're supposed to," I say. "The bad news is we're a mess, the good news is she can fix us."

We want to have our "After" pictures taken, but Ms. Merry has run out of film. The eyebrow mousse makes even Dolores look dubious.

"You're definitely a Summer," Ms. Merry says to me on her way out the door. "I know a Summer when I see one."

Dolores looks so unhappy in makeup that I consider changing the project name to Service-to-the-Unnerved.

"I'm really sorry," I say, taking library books out of my canvas bag to line up on Dolores's book cart. "My jail fashion show proposal was a terrible mistake."

Her eyes fill with tears. "It's not that," she says.

"What is it, Dolores?" I say, alarmed.

"I got convicted." She pulls a wadded piece of toilet paper out of her sleeve. It's scratchy, jail-issue toilet paper; she doesn't even have Kleenex.

I put down the books. "You got *what?*" I say.

"Convicted, for killing my husband," she cries. "I'm going up to the state prison soon as they got room for me. They're overcrowded, too."

I clutch the book cart. I feel faint. "For how long?" I say.

"Ten years," she says.

Chisholm Jim said a battered woman convicted of voluntary manslaughter could get five to ninety-nine years or life imprisonment. Her sentence could have been worse, but I've failed miserably at helping her. She never had anything, never will. She has suffered too much. I feel pierced by my glimpse into it. The wonder is that she can bear so much suffering, so many permutations of it. "Dolores," I say. "You have to appeal."

She dabs at her eyes with the wet, crumpled toilet tissue. There's nothing much left of it. I dig into my purse and give her my Kleenex purse-pack.

"They said, like, he wasn't coming at me with a deadly weapon or anything," she says. "It's like, being battered is no excuse for murder."

"But this was self-defense," I say. "He could have killed *you*."

"He punched me," she says. "If I killed him by punching him back, that would maybe have been okay."

"That's crazy," I say in disbelief.

"But now I know he's *really dead*," she says, dazed. "He must be dead, if I got convicted for killing him."

"But you knew you did," I say.

"It's like, to me he was too powerful to die," she says. "I was too helpless to have killed him."

"Oh, Dolores," I say.

"I always thought he'd kill me," she says. "I never thought it'd be me killing *him*."

I'm so upset, it seems absurd to go to my lunchtime aerobics class. I don't know whether I can make it through the rest of my life. I sit spaced-out in traffic on the freeway, in the blue Service-to-the-Unserved van. My neurotransmitters aren't transmitting, they're not making the connections they're supposed to. My mind is under construction, snarling traffic, full of detours.

I go late to aerobics anyway. I have to do my warm-up stretches by myself. If I just started dancing with everyone else, Suzi would scold me over her microphone. I wouldn't be able to take it. I bend over and look at the world from upside down. The aerobic angels bounce against the ceiling.

I'm too late to find a favorable spot, close to the front but not right in front of the mirror, not directly under one of the blaring speakers, in an open space so I won't crash into a pillar.

"Reach! Reach!" Suzi shrieks. "Suck those tummies in!" Today she wears black and fuchsia designer tights and leotard, her hair electrified, microphone to her pink mouth, the music at full blast. I stick my fingers in my ears.

"I'll bet she never gets PMS," the woman next to me says.

All I can think about is Dolores, the tragic look on her made-up face. I glimpse my own unhappy face in the mirror.

"Y'all look too serious!" Suzi screams. "It's only aerobic dancing."

Today it's total chaos—every two weeks they change the routines that take us two weeks to learn. We don't know who "they" are. New routines make us cranky. Suzi pretends she has nothing to do with it. Some people are kicking right, some are kicking left, the rest of us are just standing there trying not to get hit. Triple grapevines, hustle turns, knee-pulldowns, windmills—what kind of mind thinks these things up?

Everyone in my aerobics class suddenly looks old. We're all growing old together. The woman who cleans the locker room watches us on her lunch hour. We desperately try to learn the new routines; she laughs and slaps her thigh.

"Twenty to twenty-five?" Suzi says at the ten-second pulse-count. A few people raise their hands. "Twenty-five to thirty?" A few more people raise their hands. "I suppose the rest of you don't have any pulse at all?" she says, as upset with us as her manic cheerfulness will allow.

"Some of us are old," a man near the back gasps.

"No stopping!" she says. "If you're too high, bring yourself down."

We go from high-impact to low-impact. The lump in my throat shifts. We jog lightly in place again, clap our hands double-time over our heads to bring our pulses back up. What devotion to the body, to push and pull it into shape, to keep working on molding the clay as if it isn't finished yet. I see the bodies in the mirror, dancing. We begin to move in unison; I have no proof that one in particular is mine. Like the bouncing aerobic angels I saw from upside down, the bodies are real, but not quite real enough. We're a single being, dancing.

"Isn't this fun?" Suzi shrieks.

"No," I say. "We've had all the fun we can stand."

After work, I drive home to the Lord's Motel. The cicadas in the trees around the parking lot sound like ringing telephones. The telephone has become my enemy. It used to bring me Web and his obscene phone calls; now it takes away Gabriel in its silence.

"You let Dr. Right get *away?*" Gigi says as we all sit in St. Francis's kitchen drinking carrot juice.

"It's only been two weeks," I say, my eyes filling up.

"But he was desperate to talk to you, desperate," Gigi said. "That man jumped through hoops to get your mother's phone number from me when you were in Boston. I was impressed."

"He didn't ask you for a date?" I say. If Web had been exposed to Gigi, alone, for two minutes, I would have been history. Of course, Web is now history to me, and I'm history to Gabriel.

"Of course not," Gigi says. "Gabriel was a really great guy, gorgeous, loaded with integrity. Somehow you've managed to scare off a man much better than any you have a right to expect."

"I left a message on his answering machine but he never called back," I say.

"You'd better call him again," she says.

"I'm not going to grovel for him."

"Calling someone isn't groveling."

"I groveled so much for Web I can't take that risk," I say. "I don't know what's groveling and what isn't anymore."

"Praise God," St. Francis says, ensconced in his celibacy.

"I knew Gabriel was trouble," Barbara says. "He works twelve-hour days, two weeks at a time, and somebody's always calling him on his beeper. He's in the middle of a messy divorce, and he wears ties with whales on them." Tired of being pregnant, Barbara has so little use for men you'd think she was having a virgin birth.

"Dolores got convicted," I say, ashamed to be moaning about Gabriel when Dolores's problem is so much worse.

Gigi, Barbara, and St. Francis fall silent. The cicadas buzz louder and louder, until I have to block my ears.

"We're sorry," Gigi says finally. "It must be really hard for you, on top of losing Gabriel."

"She had made her bed and had to lay in it," I say, hearing it again just the way Dolores said it.

"What?" Gigi says.

17

Mercy

Another week goes by; Gabriel still hasn't returned my call. My confession must have seemed horrible to him. I determine to dispossess myself of him. I have a habit of thinking of him that will be hard to break. I'm bound to him by longing. My longing for him was my emotional life.

Chisholm Jim, on the other hand, calls to say we're going to court. I drive down I-45 to Galveston on the morning of my trial. It seems I've been on the road so long that everything I wear is dirty. The freeway is under eternal reconstruction; the gritty dust settles in my teeth, my hair. The lanes narrow, then the traffic slows to a stop. An accident, maybe. But where the four lanes of traffic merge into one, I see a new overpass in the making. It juts out into the sky and just stops.

I'm a nervous wreck when I walk into the Court Club in Galveston. Chisholm Jim told me to meet him here for break-fast, to plan our strategy before we go into court.

"Mornin', Judge," Chisholm Jim calls to the august types nodding to him when he lopes into the Club. He leans back and waves to them as if from the top of a bucking bronco.

"Tuna on rye toast and the jar of picante, Sammy," he says to the waiter.

"What about the dolphins?" I say.

"This is a private club," he says. "No dolphins died for this tuna."

"Just hot water for me," I say to Sammy as he flicks the white linen napkins into our laps. I brought my own teabag because places like this never have herb tea. My old way of looking at the world is about to turn upside down so I'd better eat after.

"We're in luck, sweet lady," Chisholm Jim says. "I do believe we've convinced the D.A. he can't make a case."

"How?" I say.

"Awww, none of those guys wants to be a witness. I called the D.A. and put it to him like it was, bachelor party and all."

"What about the hotel's charge against me?" I say.

"The hotel doesn't want any bad publicity from this," he says. "They're not thrilled with that kind of partying, but they came around to see you're not setting up shop on their premises."

"You mean they're dropping the charges?" I say.

He opens his tuna sandwich and pours the jar of picante sauce into it. "They'll settle for restitution for water damage to the suite below," he says. "Their insurance will cover most of it, but you'll pay their deductible."

"Prostitution restitution," I say. I'll pay it with the money the guys never offered me and I never accepted, in return for the misguided favors I never granted.

"We got a certified letter of affidavit that the hotel doesn't want to press," he says. "I took the whole package to the chief prosecutor, so this morning we'll see what happens. Anything goes wrong at showtime, we go to Plan B—no offer and acceptance, and the duress defense."

"Which defense?" I say. "I'm going on stage as two different characters and I don't know whose are my lines."

"We've got to be able to shift from one defense strategy to another as the testimony unfolds, but at the same time, we can't have so many alternative theories that we totally confuse the jury," he says. "We can't say 'We think it's this, but if it's not, we think it's that, and if you don't quite buy that, then perhaps you'll believe this.' We have to be more authoritative than that. By the time the testimony gets over to our side, we've seen how the state's testimony has unraveled, and we can choose the horse we're going to bet on."

I hyperventilate with terror.

"When it's showtime, it's showtime," he goes on. "I'll figure out what's got to come across to the jury. That's the story we've got to tell. If the prosecutor asks you a question that puts you in the hot seat, you resort back to our general theme—'I did it because he made me do it.' You don't answer the question, you go back to our defense or you say you don't know. Don't try to outsmart the prosecutor."

I try to look calm the way I did in library school while fear drew Cataloging and Classification in one ear and out the other.

"Get it? Got it? Good," Chisholm Jim says. He autographs the check, picks up his cowboy hat and his soft leather brief-case. He strides toward the door, waiters bowing toward him all the way.

I resist the urge to hold his hand while we cross the street to the courthouse. We go up in the elevator with a group of svelte young women who look like models. One of them carries a big boxed birthday cake, decorated with a frosting gavel and the name of the judge.

"How old is the son-of-a-gun?" Chisholm Jim asks them.

"Seventy," the young woman carrying the cake says.

"I knew it took him at least seventy years to get that cranky!" he says, and they all laugh.

"Who are they?" I say when we get off the elevator.

"Probation officers," he says.

Throngs of people hang around outside the courtroom—the guilty and the innocent, lawyers, victims, witnesses. Mothers nurse babies; men smoke, the sleeves of their T-shirts rolled up to show their tattoos, cigarettes stashed in the cuffs. Lawyers with briefcases dart around, step over the outstretched legs of teenage boys lounging against the wall.

Chisholm Jim sails ahead of me into the courtroom. It looks and smells like a church, with high ceilings, mahogany paneling, rows of pews. He leaves me behind the railing that divides the pews from the bar, swings through the short gate as if into a saloon. He pitches his briefcase into a chair, slaps the other attorneys on their shoulders. Young female prosecutors grin up at him. He has flirting relationships with all, but entangling alliances with none. Even the chief prosecutor looks happy to see him. He walks up and shakes Chisholm Jim's hand. They look as if they're exchanging jokes about the Super Bowl. This all has something to do with Texas politics.

Prosecutors from the district attorney's office and defense lawyers hover over the counsel table covered with case files. They're an ever-shifting mass, getting up, sitting down, playing Musical Chairs. It looks like a dinner party where no one was told where to sit and so everyone keeps looking for his place.

Chisholm Jim strides to the big table and takes a seat. He pores over a file, runs his finger down the pages. From the set of his back I can tell I'm to sit and be quiet. I hear my mother tell me to be good and not to get dirty. The courtroom pews fill up with defendants, police officers, witnesses. The hiss of lawyers whispering with their clients grows deafening.

"All files back on the counsel table," the D.A. calls out.

"All rise," the bailiff says, his gun in a patent leather holster.

A hush falls as the elderly judge walks in and takes his high-backed chair at the bench, like a high priest in his black gown. Draped on their tall stands, the American and Texas flags flank him like guardian angels. He calls the docket, an endless stream of defendants.

"Do you have an attorney?" the judge demands of the first, a pale young man shifting a baby from the crook of one arm to the other. The man fits Barbara's description of the welder who impregnated her.

"I'm s'posed to," he says, "but he ain't here yet."

I strain to hear the judge, sternly impeturbable, charge the man with assault. I worry about where the baby's mother is.

"Guilty or not guilty?" the judge says.

The man whispers earnestly to the judge.

"Guilty or not guilty?" the judge bellows. "I don't need a long speech from you. I'm going to close this case four weeks from today with or without a lawyer—it's your choice."

The baby fusses and squirms.

"Order in the court," the judge says, banging his gavel at the baby. The baby screams.

"Step this way, please," the court clerk says, and the man struggles to hold the baby and baby's bottle in one arm so he can sign a form with his other.

It's a sad parade. Driving while intoxicated, theft, child abuse, shoplifting. The prosecutors recite the charges as if intoning prayers. I'm sorry for so many people with bad taste, a sullen girl in a vinyl miniskirt and low-cut blouse, street kids in cut-offs and worn-out jogging shoes.

The bailiff stalks across the courtroom, jangling his sets of handcuffs. He opens a side door to a prisoner holding area. Just inside the door, six women sit handcuffed to their chairs.

I'd be among them if I hadn't made bail. Beyond them, about twenty men are crowded into a cell, their dark, sweaty faces peering through the bars. The stench from the closed-in cell blasts into the courtroom.

The bailiff leads a woman out of the holding area and locks the door. She reminds me of Dolores, her shoulders slumped in abject hopelessness. She stands handcuffed before the judge, in a tan jumpsuit with "Jail Property" in black letters across the back. The bailiff eyes her and shuffles a pack of cards. Whispering in his navy blue pinstripes, a prosecutor argues with the prisoner's court-appointed defense attorney. The defense attorney mumbles unhappily; the court reporter stares at him with rapt attention. How can she type that fast, and with such long, perfect fingernails?

"Are you pleading guilty because you *are* guilty and for no other reason?" the judge says to the woman.

"Yes," she says in a small voice.

I'm oppressed by my own guilt.

The bailiff takes the woman back to the locked holding cell. There's a lull, like the eye of a hurricane. Someone walks up to the judge and covers the side view of his moving mouth with a file folder. The judge lights up a cigar, it glows red on the end when he inhales. "Colleen Sweeney!" he growls.

I jump.

"Approach the bench," he says with weary impatience.

I walk dizzily toward him. I might die. Is this how Mrs. Fritz felt, tottering, reaching for a wall to steady herself?

"By the authority of the State of Texas," the prosecutor intones, "the District Attorney charges Colleen Sweeney with the following offense: Prostitution, violation of Chapter 43, Section 2 of the Texas Code of Law, Subsection (a)(1), offer to engage, agreement to engage, engaging in sexual conduct for a fee."

The word "Prostitution" rings bright red throughout the courtroom. I feel everyone's eyes on my back.

"Guilty or not guilty?" the judge says.

I feel like a piece in a jigsaw puzzle, except that all of the pieces around me have been taken away. The edges are gone, and there's plain cardboard where the picture used to be.

"Your Honor, we have a motion to dismiss," the prosecutor says.

"Give me the *nolle*," the judge says.

The prosecutor hands the judge the *nolle prosequi* form that says the D.A. wants to drop the prosecution of the case. He peers at it over the top of his glasses.

I pick a spot on the wall behind the judge but the room spins. I cling to my belief that the room isn't moving. It's an error of perception, I tell myself, a distortion from the inner ear. I listen to the voices of the people flowing by me. Everyone's in trouble. There's a terrible logic to the reasons we do things, a fundamental madness. We come before the judge not to deny our guilt, but to ask how to transcend our sins. The judge doesn't know how either. He tries to contain us and our chaos. He rolls on his chair behind the bench, picks a pen from the bouquet of them on his desk. He signs the *nolle*.

"All witnesses in the Sweeney case may go," the judge says in his gravelly voice.

I start to cry for no reason. All the absent witnesses rush like spirits through the empty spaces in my heart. Absent fathers, absent lovers, absent gods.

Chisholm Jim swings through the bar railing, cocks his head at me. "There you go, sweet lady," he says outside the courtroom, tearing off my copy of the *nolle*, signed and approved by the Court.

" 'Insufficient evidence to establish the elements of the case',"

I say, reading the line next to the checked box on the form, my eyes blurry with tears.

"So much for your legal guilt," he says. "Have you made peace with yourself?"

"My moral guilt is all mixed up with relationships, God, and the soul," I say.

"Religion is like any other facet of a person's life," he says. "Some people exercise so much, they're exercising themselves to death. People can be too religious. You've got the ones who roll on the floor and lay on hands and speak in tongues. Then you've got the ones who sit for hours—for *hours*—up in the mountains, paying some Indian thousands of dollars to tell them what they were in a previous life. It's allegedly for healing the soul—what the hell does that mean?"

"That's a good question," I say.

18

Go Texan

I wake up the next morning infinitely relieved to be going to the library instead of to jail. It's Go Texan Day, the first day of the Houston rodeo. On Go Texan, everyone in Houston dresses Western—businessmen and supermarket cashiers, computer types and waitresses, construction workers and lawyers. At the library, Joanne is squeezed into pink jeans, a pink satin cowgirl shirt with white fringe, white patent leather cowboy boots.

"You have a call on line one," Lucille says. She doesn't smirk at me any more.

"Colleen?" Gabriel says when I pick up the phone.

"Gabriel?" I say.

Neither of us can say anything else for a few moments. I know he's still there; I feel how present he is, even over the phone.

"I'm sorry I haven't called—my divorce went to trial," Gabriel says finally. "I've been to hell and back with Felicity."

"I wish you had let me know," I say, in the most dignified tone I know.

"I should have," he says. "But it was something I had to go through alone."

"Congratulations," I say. Is that what you say when people get divorced?

"I'd really like to see you," he says. "Would you go to the rodeo with me?"

Gabriel picks me up after work. He's dressed Western in jeans, boots, and white cowboy hat, except for his whale tie. In any case, the blue tie with white whales is color-coordinated with his outfit.

"How many whale ties have you got?" I say.

"Whales are an endangered species," he says.

For days, the rodeo has been advertising free shuttles from the malls, in the vain hope that the entire city won't try to park at the Astrodome. Someone once came up with a mass transit plan for Houston, but he was exiled to New York. Gabriel and I go early enough to park easily at the Astrodome but we're uneasy with one another. I'm nervous because there seems so much to hash out. Being with him reminds me of all the things I like about him—his serious intelligence, his kindness, his quiet sense of humor. I allow myself to feel how much I've missed him.

We have time before the rodeo starts to see the livestock show and some of the contests in the Astrohall. We walk through the happy chaos of farm equipment, Indian jewelry, stalls of cows, sheep, and chickens, booths where you can get your cowboy hat cleaned and shaped. The air is heavy with rodeo smells—barbecue and homemade fudge, spilled beer, manure, sawdust.

"So how've you been?" Gabriel says.

"Okay," I say, trying to read his face. "The prostitution charges against me were dropped."

"Great!" he says. "How did that happen?" He raises his

eyebrows at me. I read somewhere that raising one's eyebrows is a variation on a smile.

When I tell him, his face clouds over, as if he wishes he hadn't asked. He falls silent, withdrawing into himself again the way he did when we discussed this after the dinner I cooked for him. "I guess I still have a hard time with your being willing to do it in the first place," he says after a while.

A woman in a long denim skirt holds her orange yardstick across the aisle. We pause while a rancher leads a line of cattle to the judging arena. I feel judged by Gabriel.

"I wasn't 'willing to do it,' " I say, hurt. "Web got me into the situation but I didn't go through with the actual prostitution."

"Did Web get you into compromising situations often?" he says.

"Too often, but that's all over now," I say. "I'm not seeing Web anymore."

"This is all very confusing," he says.

This isn't going well. Gabriel and I are having a lovers' quarrel before we ever got to be lovers. The last steer lumbers by; the denim-skirted woman raises her yardstick. We walk again down the aisle. "This is like a *Who's Who* of animals," I say to change the subject, reading the breeds of cattle on their stalls.

Gabriel doesn't respond. In the auction arena, bidders lock horns to buy the champion steer, thirteen hundred pounds. He goes for $221,000. The judge slaps the steer on his rump.

"What happens to him?" I say.

"He goes to slaughter at Texas A & M," Gabriel says. "The meat goes to market and the proceeds go to charity."

"The karma of that is a little hard to sort out," I say.

We shuffle disconsolately together down the sawdust aisles

looking for something vegetarian at the booths vending sausage, fajitas, boudin, beef jerky, smoked turkey thighs.

"Whatever happened to the four basic food groups?" I say.

"Texas has only three—beef, pork, and link," he says.

We settle for corn dogs, eating them from sticks. We watch the horseshoe pitching for a few minutes, then head for the fiddlers' contest. The bleachers are packed. A teenage girl in red gingham fiddles while she flirts with her back-up guitarist.

"What about you?" I say to Gabriel. "How are you?"

"I'm doing better now," he says. "Now that my divorce is final."

The next fiddling contestant, a little boy in slicked hair, plays a mournful version of "Three Blind Mice."

"What about your son?" I say.

"Felicity got custody, but I get visitation rights," he says, cheering up a bit. "First, third, and fifth weekends, every other Christmas, Thanksgiving, Easter, Halloween—every other everything."

"That's wonderful," I say. "What a relief it must be."

"I'm *ecstatic*," he says. "Felicity got practically everything, but I escaped with my son and my life."

"The winner will receive a plane ticket to Lubbock, a real nice gold buckle, and a whole lot o' money," the announcer says before the fiddlers' play-offs.

"You can always get more *stuff*," I say. "Stuff has a way of just sticking to people."

The fiddling contestants take so long to draw for their positions that Gabriel and I leave so we won't miss the pig races in the Swine Arena. On the way, Gabriel stops to have his photo taken on the stuffed bucking Brahman bull. He mounts in his jeans and white hat, throws his leg over the bull. He holds on with one hand, leans back, throws the other arm up in the air as if he has been doing this all his life.

I stare up at him. Why would he want his photo taken on a stuffed bull? Maybe it's his divorce portrait. Maybe he wants a picture of himself trying to stay with our relationship, such as it is. Why does he act as if I'm trying to throw him, when he's the one trying to throw *me*? The crowd presses around me. The photographer takes an eternity setting up the photo. At last, he takes Gabriel's picture. In the pop of the flashbulb, I'm horrified to think I see Web in the crowd, standing in front of a booth of registered longhorn semen.

"What's the matter?" Gabriel says when he's back at my side, looking into my stricken face.

"For a second I thought I saw Web," I say.

"What would he be doing here?" he says.

"That corn dog must have made me hallucinate," I say.

"How do you feel about Web now?" he blurts.

"I got in touch with my anger, but he doesn't even make me angry anymore," I say. "I just feel a vague sort of sadness."

"That's a good sign," he says. "Sadness comes after anger in the seven stages of grieving. I'm going through the same thing with my divorce."

"I thought anger came after sadness," I say.

"It doesn't really matter what order we do it in, as long as we do it," he sighs.

By the time we get to the Swine Arena, the pig races are over. The woman at the door misreads my sorrowful countenance. "Honey, the pig races weren't really that great this year," she says.

We wander through the agricultural equipment exhibitions—hay-lifters and tractors, barn kits, stock tanks, feed troughs. There's even a computerized herd-improvement system. In one exhibit area, the Future Farmers of America compete in livestock, dairy, horses, meat-carcass grading, mohair. We stop to watch a sheep-to-shawl demonstration.

"That sheep was taken to the cleaners," Gabriel says of the bewildered naked animal. "Felicity must have got hold of him."

"How do you feel now about Felicity?" I say.

He just shakes his head, the way a man does when he doesn't trust his voice. He presses his lips together, refusing to talk about it. He kissed me once with those lips. I feel a stab of love.

We move on to a Future Farmer who has just won a scholarship for her grand champion boar. The boar roots around in the dirt, then plops down contentedly.

"Will he perish for his efforts?" I ask her.

"Oh, no," she says. "This is a pig with a future. He'll come back to the farm to sire. The champion barrow—the neutered male—will be slaughtered."

In the Children's Barnyard, surrounded by piglets, calves, chicks, and children, a ewe gives birth to lambs.

"Did Barbara have her baby?" Gabriel says.

"Not yet, but she will any minute," I say. "St. Francis is lobbying for a non-dairy alternative to breast milk."

Gabriel manages a laugh. It floats over the country music as we walk out of the Astrohall's livestock show toward the Astrodome for the rodeo.

The rodeo show has a sell-out crowd. Our seats are practically backstage, over the chutes where the bulls stomp and snort. Next to the chutes, those riding in the Grand Entrance parade gather to wait for the signal to begin. We look down on the skittish horses, the rodeo officials running about with cellular phones, the socialites flapping in their long designer dusters and big hair. Cowboys line the rails, doing leg stretches like macho ballerinas.

Venders run up and down the steep steps between the stands with rodeo programs thick as telephone books, peanuts and ice cream and beer. Pre-teen girls in makeup and tight jeans beg their boyfriends to buy them stuffed puppies and heart-shaped balloons. Gabriel buys me a pair of Texas-shaped sunglasses.

"Have you seen your son yet?" I say.

"Next weekend," he says. "I'm counting the minutes."

"I'm sure he'll be thrilled to see *you*," I say.

The rodeo announcer takes his place on the grandstand; the band leader raises his baton. The Grand Entrance begins. Section by section, the crowd stands as the Sheriff's Mounted Posse passes by with the American and Texas flags. Then the Mayor on horseback, horse-drawn buggies of major sponsors, haywagons full of 4-H kids. The marching band plays "Deep in the Heart of Texas"; baton twirlers in short, fringed skirts lead a Brahman bull and a longhorn steer. Then come the veterinary paramedics, floats for beer and ranch-style beans, Little Mr. and Miss Go Texan. Conestoga wagons and Native Americans and the Texas Sweethearts in red satin. The furni-ture-store float with sponsors dressed up as mattresses. The Say No to Drugs float, the Cowboys of Yesteryear, and the Astronauts of Tomorrow. And trail riders from all across Texas, followed by the Aggie Poop Patrol shoveling up horse manure. The crowd applauds.

After the Grand Entrance exits, a preacher offers the open-ing prayer. Tiny on the distant grandstand, his earnest face looms on the wide video screens. Then, all sixty thousand of us stand for "The Star-Spangled Banner." With "the rockets' red glare," firecrackers explode at the top of the Astrodome. The shower of red sparks lights up the darkened arena.

"Was that American or what?" the announcer hoots.

The first bucking bronco bursts from the chute. The rider tries to stay on for eight seconds, synchronizing his movements with the horse's bucking any way he can. He holds onto the thick rein with one hand, keeping his free hand clear of the horse.

"The best riders have a strong hand and a good sense of balance," Gabriel says.

"I hope they've completed their families," I say, watching the next bounce violently in his saddle.

The announcer tells the crowd where each cowboy's from—South Dakota or Arizona or Oklahoma—then gives a breathless account of the ride. The riders all lose their hats; some are thrown from the horse after only a few seconds.

"You gotta quit gittin' off your horse that way," the announcer jokes to a cowboy lying breathless on the ground. The pick-up men on horseback help him up and out of the arena. The rodeo clown races around the arena in a barrel pulled by a harnessed rooster, to give the crowd time to recover from having the wind knocked out of it. The cowboy is on oxygen.

"This is so *intense*," I say.

"It is, isn't it?" Gabriel says. He turns to look me in the eye. Then he looks away.

This was to be my dream date with Gabriel; now it seems it could be my last. This is the fastest I've ever screwed up a relationship. I feel I've fallen off the bronco before the chute opened. Dolores pops into my mind. I've been given the second chance that she has been denied. I tried to make a mission of her, but she was the one who helped *me*. Whatever happens with Gabriel, I'll land on my feet.

"Dolores got convicted," I tell Gabriel.

"I'm really sorry to hear that," Gabriel says, after a pause.

"She's going to the women's prison at Gatesville," I say.

"For how long?" he says.

"Ten years," I say, with a heavy heart.

A haze hangs over the enormous arena in the lull before

the bull riding, the most dangerous event. The crowd stamps restlessly. I feel suspended, as if given a wide view of something both distant and intimate.

A red light pops on over the chute of the first bull riding contestant. The announcer's voice has an urgent edge when he tells us the name of the cowboy, where he's from, what prizes he has won. The wide-screen video shows a close-up of the cowboy's hand gripping the manila rope behind the bull's shoulders. The bull bucks out of the chute, desperate to throw him. One arm in the air, the cowboy stays close up on his handhold, his legs clutching the bull's rib cage. The crowd breathes a collective sigh of relief when the cowboy makes it to the end of the eight seconds, slides from the bull and runs for his life.

"The bulls weigh from eleven hundred pounds to one ton," the announcer says before the next contestant. "The leaning weight of one of these bulls can break a rider's legs before he's out of the chute."

I could pass out from terror for the cowboys, from the mix of joy and pain at being here with Gabriel. My capacitors are overloaded. The red light comes on over the next contestant's chute. The bull charges out, spinning.

"Spinners are dangerous—the rider can be trampled if he falls to the inside of the bull," Gabriel groans.

The cowboy hits the ground on all fours. The bull lowers his head and hooks his horns under the cowboy, throws him high into the air.

The huge crowd roars to its feet.

"Where are the pick-up men?" I scream to Gabriel in the din.

"They can't use pick-up men in this," he shouts back. "The bull will fight a man on horseback as soon as one on foot."

The rodeo clown pops half out of his barrel in his face paint, red and white polka dots, suspenders. He's the cowboy's only hope. The furious bull seems distracted for a moment, then heads for the cowboy staggering to his feet.

"I'm gonna shish-ke-bab this one," the announcer speaks for the bull. His voice reverberates throughout the Dome.

The clown jumps from his barrel. In a cloud of dust, he must look like an apparition to the bull—so small, so bright, so fearless. He distracts the bull for the seconds it takes the cowboy to stagger to the fence and be dragged over it. The bull charges the clown, who dives backwards into his barrel, rump first. The crowd goes mad with relief.

"It's all so violent," I say, barely holding back my tears.

At intermission, the crowd streams toward the concession stands for peanuts, ice cream, and beer. Our entire row crawls past us, over our knees. I feel as if we're the only people in church not going to Communion. Left alone, Gabriel and I suffer through an awkward silence.

"Would you like another corn dog?" Gabriel says, finally.

"I'm not hungry," I say. I'm starved for some sign that he still cares for me.

"Neither am I," he says.

What did he mean, back at the livestock show, when he said he found it all too confusing—my arrest, the dropping of the charges, my relationship with Web, the end of my relationship with Web? I feel so different from myself as an exotic dancer, I don't see why he can't tell just by looking at me. "Are you afraid I'll take off my clothes and dance at the rodeo?" I say.

"I don't know *what* you'll do," he says, startled. "That part of you is very disturbing to me."

A man drives a little truck around the arena, cleaning up manure after all the broncos, horses, bulls. Gabriel and I watch as if it's the most fascinating thing we've ever seen in our lives.

"Then maybe we should go home," I fume.

"I think it's unlikely we're going to solve all this tonight," he says. "Let's just stay and watch the rest of the rodeo."

People return from the concession stands, crawling back the other way over our knees.

"Why did you invite me to the rodeo if you're so ambivalent about me?" I say.

"I thought maybe you'd like to come," he says. "I thought we might have a good time together."

"*Are* we having a good time?" I say.

"Beats the heck out of visiting you in jail," he says.

"You were going to visit me?" I say.

"Of course," he says.

"But why, if you don't care about me?" I say, taken aback.

"I'm upset because I *do* care about you," he says, looking straight into my eyes.

"I may never be able to explain to you why I did those things with Web," I say.

"We just have to get around it," he says. "Why did I marry Felicity? Why did I get divorced? It's not something you're ever going to really understand. I don't understand it myself. We each know we want something different from what we had before. We don't have any experience of it, that's why it's—"

"Frightening?" I say.

"Let's just hang in there," he says.

Stagehands push an enormous rotating stage on wheels to the middle of the arena, anchor it, and plug in dozens of electrical connections. Light and sound technicians test equipment for the upcoming performance by the country superstar, Chuck Wagon. Chuck's a homegrown Texan who has wowed the country music world with Grammys, number one singles, albums of the year.

The audience is beside itself with anticipation. The video crew pans the crowd. Gabriel and I are shaken to see ourselves as a couple up on the wide screen. It's as if Mrs. Fritz, wherever she is, had something to do with it.

"That's as official as it gets," Gabriel says, breaking into a smile. The dimple between his eyes reappears.

The lights go down on his smile; a hush falls over the crowd. In the darkened corner from which Chuck will emerge, the Texas flag bursts into fireworks. With a few chords from his biggest hit, Chuck rides into the arena in his trademark gold chuckwagon drawn by a gold stretch limo. He waves his gold hat and his adoring fans go wild. Flashbulbs pop to the pulse of the music.

Chuck steams up the crowd with cheatin' songs. With his swinging fiddles and steel guitar he puts the twang back in country. Our hearts follow him through cowboy anthems and Western swing, ballads, and honky tonk. He kicks back into his romantic numbers. The lighting shifts from red to green to blue. The gold figures of Chuck's tight band revolve with him on the rotating stage. They're all so tiny and far away. All we see of Chuck is his sad smile, grinning from his hat to his sunbelt. His yearning voice fills the emptiness of the Dome.

"Something in him is aching to get out," Gabriel says. The rough blond hairs on the back of his hand brush my wrist as he seeks my hand and finds it.

We slip out together. Sweet, faint strains of country western music follow us out to the parking lot. Hand in hand, we walk through acres of empty cars. From the other side of the vast parking lot, we turn to look back at the apocalyptic shape of the Astrodome. Is it a silver flying saucer? A solidified mushroom cloud? Nothing about my relationship with Gabriel is certain, but everything seems possible.

"What does it take to really love someone, and to be loved?" I say.

"It's like with the rodeo riders," Gabriel says, after a pause. He folds me into his arms, holds me close. "It takes a lot of try. It takes a lot of want-to."

I'm in the arms of a man who has no wish to harm me, about to be kissed by the man I wish to kiss. My insides are doing things I just don't understand. Mrs. Fritz said that. I find myself on the other side of the country western songs—no longer the cheatin' side, but the heavenly, glorious side of love.

"How do you feel?" Gabriel says. He kisses me for his answer.

A billow of music reaches us, on a fresh breeze. He kisses the breath out of me, while I try to figure out how to say I've never before felt this happy, this loved.

"Texan," I say.

19

Praise God

Killer bees are migrating up the Rio Grande Valley, north into Texas. The Valley is lush with water and wildflowers, the spread of bees much wider than anyone expected. County after county is quarantined as more hives are found, more people stung to death. Killer bee books for the inmates are now out of the question, but they've lost interest in them anyway. Instead, they want books on killer whales.

Lieutenant Sprunt calls to tell me that Dolores is about to be taken to the women's state prison at Gatesville. I rush to the jail in the blue Service-to-the-Unserved van. I'm just in time to say goodbye. Dolores stands outside the front door with solemn dignity, at the end of a line of five other hand-cuffed women. She manages a weak smile when she sees me. Lieutenant Sprunt nods at me, distracted while he and the van driver sign off on each other's paperwork.

I give Dolores a news article about recent state legislation for review of the cases of women convicted for killing the men who abused them. The review process includes a study of the women's files and documentation. The parole board panel can recommend clemency, parole, or even pardon.

Dolores clutches the scrap of newspaper with the fingers of one handcuffed hand. "I'm writin' down my story," she tells me. "I'm waitin' for my chance to tell it to the Texas Board of Pardons and Paroles."

My heart hurts, thinking how painful it will be for her to document her abuse. "Battered women's syndrome is a kind of post-traumatic stress disorder," I say.

"If I ever get out, I'm going to work in counseling to help women like me," she says. "I don't much care about being a manicurist anymore."

"You helped me see I was in a self-destructive relationship, Dolores," I say.

"Don't shoot him," she says.

"It was only emotional battering," I say.

"Don't wound him, even," she says.

Her face seems softer and paler, as if she's all cried out. I'm thankful to see she finally got new glasses. Someone has chopped at her hair but not succeeded in subduing its wildness. It glints red from the roots, it crackles before my eyes. In the Texas sun, it really looks on fire.

A corrections officer opens the van door. The six women shuffle toward it, step up into it one at a time.

"Well, 'bye now," Dolores says, her lower lip trembling. "Thanks for the books, and everything."

"Goodbye, Dolores," I say, choking back tears. I hug her, but her handcuffs prevent her from hugging me back.

The hug makes the guard nervous, as if I might be passing her a weapon. He steps forward, herds her into the prison van behind the others. He slams and locks the door, goes around to the driver's side, and climbs in.

Dolores looks out, her face ghostly through the van's grated window. The sunlight casts crisscrossed shadows on her face. I'll miss her so much.

Lieutenant Sprunt stands next to me, his arms folded across his chest. "I'll have a hard time finding a trusty to replace her as jail librarian," he says. "It's a damn shame she got convicted. Battered women who kill, like Dolores, tend to be model prisoners. They adapt, they don't have problems with authority, they aren't repeat offenders."

Web calls me at the library, for the first time since my arrest. "I'm on the pay phone in front of the Lord's Motel," he says.

At first I think it's a bad joke, that he's really on a ship in some distant ocean. Then, with a sinking feeling, I realize he really is at the Lord's Motel. I can't believe his nerve. "You'd better be gone by the time I get home," I say.

"Don't be like that," he says.

"I got *arrested* because of you."

"Think of it as an *adventure*," he says.

"I think of it as sexual suicide," I say.

A long pause. I can almost see him staring at the phone.

"I told you I'd love you if I could, but I can't," he says, after a while.

"Find someone else not to love," I say. Felicity comes to mind.

His next pause sounds hurt.

"You've found someone else," he says eventually.

I don't say anything. I can't have a relationship with Gabriel or anyone until I get over my rage at Web and recover my self-esteem. That's what the self-help books say; whether it's like that in real life is another question.

"You were supposed to tell me when you were ready for a serious relationship," he says, sounding sincere for once.

I'm speechless. "Goodbye, Web," I say finally.

I rush home after work to the Lord's Motel to see whether

Barbara has had the baby yet. St. Francis has spent days baby-proofing Barbara's apartment, but now he lies on the floor of his bedroom with his head on his meditation cushion. The cats press their little faces against the window.

"Starvation," Barbara says. "I'm eating for two and he's starving himself to death."

"I'm fasting," St. Francis says. "God's telling me not to eat even avocados or oranges until this baby is born."

"God's telling you you've screwed up your digestive system and you'd better eat a lot more than avocados and oranges," Gigi says.

"True friends wouldn't tempt me," he says.

"We can't just let you die, St. Francis," I say.

"I have eternal life," he says.

"Nevertheless, you're dangerously close to dropping the body," I say, turning on his juicer. I make him some juice and hold the jelly jar glass to his lips.

"Do you know that people are buying electric forks?" he says, reluctantly swallowing a sip. "So they can cultivate gluttony and laziness at the same time?"

"God doesn't care about electric forks, St. Francis," I say.

"The United States is a lower chakra culture," he says, "but there are pockets of the higher energy centers like compassion and wisdom."

"Where?" I say. "In Kansas? Nebraska?"

"We're trying to move from the power chakra up to the heart chakra, at least," he says.

"How was your dream date at the rodeo with Gabriel?" Gigi whispers to me outside our apartments at the top of the stairs.

"He cares about me, but I think he's a little afraid of me," I say. "He knows I'm capable of going too far."

"A *little* afraid?" Gigi says. "He should be *petrified*." She roots in her purse for a tiny foil-wrapped square of nicotine gum. She unwraps it with her long red fingernails, pops the gum into her mouth. She savors it as if it's an escargot. Then she pushes it to one side of her mouth, takes a cigarette from her purse and lights it with a new engraved sterling silver lighter. "You have to show him the other parts of yourself," she says. "He needs to be convinced that there's more to you than that."

"Isn't nicotine gum a substitute for smoking?" I say.

"I'm easing my way into it," she says, dragging and chewing. "Besides, Jack gave me my silver lighter before he knew I got my gum prescription."

"I hope Gabriel doesn't turn out to be repressed, like Henry, your x," I say.

"Henry was hopeless," she says. "Gabriel's a normal man with a normal problem and you're the woman for the job."

"He does seem to want to work things out," I say.

"Then give him a break," she says. "He just got divorced—he's all freaked out."

"You're telling me," I say. "He'll have to discover for himself that, unlike Felicity, I'm a loving, trustworthy woman."

Gigi has a coughing fit. She doubles up, hangs over the banister. I pound her on the back, worried that she'll choke on her gum.

St. Francis opens his door at the bottom of the stairs. "Is something on fire?" he says.

"No," Gigi calls down, scooping the smoke back up into our hallway.

"Lucky for you, St. Francis is too weak from fasting to climb the stairs," I whisper to Gigi when he goes back into his apartment.

"Is Gabriel dating anyone else?" she says.

"I have no idea," I say.

She puts out her cigarette, pushes the gum to the other side of her mouth. "They have nicotine patches now to wear on your arm," she says. "Do you think Gabriel would prescribe them for me?"

"Why don't you ask your own doctor?" I say.

"He won't let me smoke and chew nicotine gum *and* wear a patch," she says.

"With good reason," I say.

"This is going to be a tough one," she says. "Gabriel's going to be a challenge. You already have something major to overcome."

"You talk as if he's the last man in the world," I say.

"He *is*," she says. "Unless you're ready for video dating."

I gasp. Gigi is enough to give me a panic disorder.

"Gabriel is your *last chance*," Gigi says as I retreat into my apartment. "Don't *fuck it up*."

St. Francis fasts throughout rodeo week as Barbara grows still bigger. She's bursting out of her suits for pregnant businesswomen. The bank gives her a baby shower. I give her an environmentally friendly diaper service, and Gigi gives her a car seat so she can take the baby to the bank. Barbara's mother sends her a bassinet from Neiman Marcus, then visits from Waco. She looks as if she intends to have a talk with the baby's father.

Barbara introduces her mother to St. Francis. "This is not the baby's father," Barbara says matter-of-factly, "but the baby does have a father."

Her mother gives her an odd look, then goes back to Waco.

St. Francis has never fasted this long before, but then, he has never waited for a baby. He says he feels weak at first, dragging out the garbage, then he gets used to it. He hugs us weakly; we're careful when we hug him back. He goes out in the parking lot and throws handfuls of seed at the pigeons. The seed splashes down and the birds splash up, then the birds settle down on the seeds. He flaps thick brown pieces of raw liver down on the back step for the cats. "They'd eat your hand off if you let them," he says.

He worries that he's letting this part of the mind of God slip out of balance. It's as if the hidden baby is taking over the building. But how would he struggle against the baby's quiet growth?

Barbara begins to lose her composure; she's ready for this to be over. "My feet are three sizes larger," she groans. "Even my contact lenses don't fit. My gums are swollen, I can hardly get in the door of my apartment, and I can't concentrate on processing loans." This last seems to bother her the most.

"This baby *has* to be born soon," I reassure her. It's two weeks late and we're all wondering what it's doing up there.

"It's waiting for the proper alignment of the planets," St. Francis says. "It doesn't want to be an Aquarius, it wants to be a Pisces."

This pushes Barbara over the edge. "What about *the mother?*" she says. "What kind of horoscope do I have to have to have this baby?"

We all go to the hospital on the day Barbara's horoscope says she should balance her checkbook, mow the lawn, and start a do-it-yourself project.

Barbara's hysteria peaks on her way into the birthing room. "I don't know how to do this," she protests.

"It'll be fine," I tell her. "You grew up on a farm."

"It will serve you all right if I have a calf or a chicken!" she gasps.

Gigi and I sit in the waiting room and wait. I once asked

my mother what it was like, expecting me. "I didn't know *what* to expect," she said. "I didn't know any babies or people who had them. I'd hardly even *seen* a baby."

It's an easy birth. The baby slips out of Barbara and swims away into the vast spaciousness of the doctor's arms. We don't see it, but we hear it. It sounds like a "Yee-haw!" Gigi and I look at each other.

"Was that Barbara or the doctor?" I say to Gigi.

St. Francis looks up from his meditation. "I pray it wasn't the baby," he says.

The doctor comes out into the waiting room. Laboring under the misconception that St. Francis is the father, the doctor makes his way toward him. "A fine, healthy little cowboy," the doctor says, gently placing his hand on St. Francis's shoulder. "Born on the final day of the rodeo—how 'bout *that?*"

"Praise God," St. Francis says.

About the Author

Gail Donohue Storey was born in Cambridge, Massachusetts. She has worked as a librarian and as administrative director of the Creative Writing Program at the University of Houston. Her short fiction has been published in many magazines and quarterlies, including *Chicago Review, Fiction, Gulf Coast, Intro,* and *The North American Review. The Lord's Motel* is her first novel. Ms. Storey lives with her husband, a hospice physician, in Houston, Texas.